DARK FEVER

JONAH SEVERIN

Black Rose Writing | Texas

ISBN: 978-1-68433-675-3
PUBLISHED BY BLACK ROSE WRITING
www.blackrosewriting.com

Printed in the United States of America
Suggested Retail Price (SRP) $17.95

Dark Fever is printed in Garamond

*As a planet-friendly publisher, Black Rose Writing does its best to eliminate unnecessary waste to reduce paper usage and energy costs, while never compromising the reading experience. As a result, the final word count vs. page count may not meet common expectations.

DARK
FEVER

PROLOGUE

The sun beats down on us after we wrap up the yardwork. My grandfather drives the riding mower up the slope into the trailer. I help him close it before we clamber into his blood-red Dodge Ram. He shifts it into drive as we get onto the interstate, tuning in to nothing but the noises of the world around us. There are no words uttered between us, indeed after we devoted all day doing landscaping for the elderly people my grandpa always went out of his way to serve in stages of need. I relax in the passenger seat as all becomes surreal, serving me a sense of tranquility. My grandfather looks over at me, giving me that smile he consistently possesses, the beam that invariably causes me to feel at home.

But when we drag into the driveway, I know home isn't where I prefer to be.

"You alright, child?" My grandfather finally talks. He has always been a man of few words.

I don't look at him as I'm struggling to fight back tears. "James? James, look at me."

Releasing a hefty murmur, I spin to him.

"What's wrong?"

"Nothing."

"Doesn't look like nothing. Out with it," he says sternly.

I take another look at the house, knowing what rests on the other side of the front door, that sense of dread seizing control over me. That dread, that knowing, is the reason my mother has begun taking me to therapy.

At least that is what she tells me every time I ask her why I have to go, which is every single time. What I don't question is why she seems frantic when we get there, but calm once we leave. She probably thinks I don't see it. I know she won't give me credit for picking up something like that.

She doesn't give me credit for anything.

Not like she used to.

I know it's my father's fault.

"No, it's really nothing," I say, trying to be as reassuring as possible. I know my grandfather is a good man, which is why I don't want him involved with what occurs once I walk through the front door.

My mother doesn't want her dad to see her the way she is.

I don't want her mad at me.

Because if she's mad at me, then my father will get mad at me. He will take that anger out on me. But not only me. My siblings as well. Being the older brother, I have to protect them as much as possible.

"I love you, grandpa," I say, climbing out of the truck,

"Hey, James!"

He calls after me. I turn to him as he climbs out of the truck. He walks over and hugs me. "You know you can tell me anything, right?"

"Yes," I lie, because I know I must.

In a way, I'm protecting him. Though I would like nothing more than to have him, or someone, anyone, to protect me.

1

The bedroom is filled with the opening rifts of "Are You Gonna Go My Way" by Lenny Kravitz. I try to get creative with the alarm on my phone to ensure that I get up at 6AM. It's Monday, which means it is the beginning of yet another shitty work week, at my shitty job, which means I don't want to get up. I reach over to press snooze but then my daughter, Sophie, sits up like the serial killers do in the movies just when everyone believes them to be dead.

I know I'm getting up.

I rise to my feet, pick up the little lady up from the bed where she passed out between my wife Braelynn and I the night before, and shuffle to the kitchen, still trying to gain my vision. I place Sophie into a chair, then pop waffles in the toaster. Coffee is made. The aroma hits my nostrils and I can't wait to taste it.

I normally hate coffee, but ever since becoming a social worker/husband/father, it has become my best friend.

I sit at the table with Sophie, giving her waffles and juice as I hold my superhero coffee mug in between both hands, not feeling anything like a superhero. I am powerless. I cannot save the world, which is something I should have paid attention to in college.

The other students and I, we all thought going into social work would make us heroes. That we would be able to save lives. That we would be able to change the world for the better. We would make children happy, and we would help families work through their issues, becoming better and stronger.

But that hasn't been the case.

Not at all.

Once the last sliver of coffee hits the bottom of my belly, I get clothes out for Sophie so she can get ready as my wife finishes up her morning workout. I shower and I don't feel like shaving today. I make sure I look somewhat presentable, but I want the world to see how I feel when they look at me. My wife greets me with a hug and a kiss as she enters the only bathroom. Feeling her next to me provides me some warmth and comfort, which lasts as long as the hug.

My wife is a social worker like me. She enjoys what she does, and I wish I could say the same thing. She's able to turn it off, separating home life from work. That's a skill I haven't quite mastered.

Not sure if I ever will.

Braelynn kisses Sophie goodbye, telling her to have a good day. She is not Sophie's mother, but she treats her like a daughter, nonetheless. I kiss her once again, doing all that I can to feel that warmth and comfort one more time before hitting the road. As I walk hand in hand with my daughter, the rest of the world slows down, as do I, trying to cherish every moment I have with her.

After dropping her off at the school, I get in the car and I wait for a few moments. I look at the reflection of my eyes. They are tired and worn, like the rest of me feels. I let out a heavy sigh before backing out of the driveway and heading to work.

The last place I want to be.

During the drive in, I leave myself shrouded in silence. No radio. No heat, despite the biting winter cold sneaking into the car. Just quiet, except for my mind. It gets as loud as the heavy metal I normally listen to when I try to amp myself up for another day at work. I wonder what happened to make me feel the way I feel. So defeated. So against the world around me. So against trying to save it.

I just know that, going into work, I will do all that I can to avoid going out into the field. I'm so sick of dealing with people, be it my coworkers or the clients we try to help.

I know that people are going to do whatever it is that they want, no matter how many rules are put into place. No matter how many times you try to provide the tools they could use to better their situation and, in my case, get their children back.

I work within the foster care system in New York. It's been a shit job since day one and has only gotten worse as time has gone on. Trying to help parents and kids who won't help themselves, plus a supervisor who makes it seem like I'm back in Germany as part of the Hitler regime. There are days that half a bottle of Jack just doesn't cut it.

My phone buzzes as I take a seat at my desk.

My first immediate thought is that I haven't even been here five fucking minutes and shit is already hitting the fan.

I consider not picking up, but it continues ringing and I just want it to stop.

Pressing the phone to my ear, swallowing the sigh trying to escape my lungs, "Hello?"

"Hope you're having a good morning," I hear the voice on the other end state. It's one of the foster parents I work with, Dave.

"I could say that, but something tells me it's going to turn to shit really quick."

"Quentin...uh...he ran away. Left a note and he took a bunch of his stuff."

My heart sinks and my stomach turns every way that it shouldn't. "What did the note say?"

Dave sighs deeply into the phone. "It says that he had been talking with one of his friends about going to California and that we don't need to come look for him. That he's tired of being told what he can and can't do."

I run my hand over my face and through my hair, my mind already conjuring up the worst.

"I've already notified law enforcement, and I gave them your number. They said they'd assign the case to a detective in order to track him down. I feel he'll be back here in a week."

Feeling the worry on my face, I close my eyes to try to push it out. "I hope you're right."

I end the call and lean back in my chair. Panic sets in as I shake my head, trying to believe my own words as I repeat that everything will be okay.

I go into my supervisor Cindy's office and notify her of the news. Cindy looks like more of a mess than I do, with her bathroom shoes, wrinkled pants and shirt stretched out to her knees. "Have you done everything else you have to do?"

Everything will be okay.

I'm not in a good mood and Quentin running away hasn't made it any better so I'm ready to explode and it's not even 8:30. "I just got the news, Cindy. Figured I'd tell you before I did anything else, but I'll take care of the

3

paperwork," I say as I make my way out of her office, part of me wondering why the fuck I went in there to begin with.

Everything will be okay.

I must alert the state's missing children's network, which is a form I have to fill out electronically. Once that is done, I head out to the Department of Juvenile Justice to inform them about Quentin and file a runaway petition with a woman named Becky.

She says, "I hope he turns up. I'd hate for him to get caught up in this human trafficking mess."

"I hope so, too."

Everything will be okay. Everything will be okay. Everything will be okay.

I meet with Detective Devin Browning at my office when I return. He is waiting for me in the lobby. We shake hands before I lead him to my office. He takes a moment to assess it, probably thinking that I'm some sort of bum, but with all that has happened today, I don't have time or motivation to give a shit.

He gives me the rundown of what he does before asking me for basic information about Quentin. I give him all that I know in regard to his appearance and history before Browning asks, his voice sounding like he's been chewing gravel, "So, do you know of anyone in California? The foster parent stated the juvenile would be going out there."

"No."

"Did he mention friends out there that you know of?"

"No."

"Are you sure?"

"Positive."

We stare at one another. I can tell he is trying to figure me out, because it is the same thing I'm doing with him. In this line of work, you assess everyone, and develop a profile in your head, which is filled with biases.

"So, what do you think has happened with the juvenile?"

I shrug, "I'm not sure. Dave told me what he took with him. I think he's probably on a friend's couch somewhere."

"But you don't know of any friends?"

I shake my head, "No. He never really mentioned friends. The fact that he ran away is still new to me. He never gave off any indication he was unhappy. I know that he didn't like the fact that I had to lay down some rules when it came to driving since he liked to pop pills and smoke weed. I told him that I didn't want anything to happen to him or anyone else while he was behind the wheel."

Browning makes notes, just as I do during a home visit. Never really taking his eyes off of me, just as I do with clients, but his hand guiding the pen across the paper.

"So, what happens now?" I ask.

"I'll send out flyers with his name and picture around the area. If you have numbers for parents or any other family, I'd like to have those."

"I can do that," I say, leaning down and grabbing Quentin's file. "Do you have a lot of luck when it comes to finding missing teens?" I ask, trying my best to not show that I'm looking for some sort of comfort. I want to hug my wife and child again. I need it.

Browning leans back and runs his hand over his short hair, looking more like a soldier than anything else. "Oh, I always find them. I've never had a case where I haven't. But," he pauses, "that doesn't mean they are always alive or in good condition."

I say nothing.

I just frown as my mind screams.

Everything will be okay. Everything will be okay. Everything will be okay.

2

The evening runs away from me when I get home, just as it always does. Evenings spent preparing dinner while my wife does a workout or cleans the rest of the house. We eat dinner and watch a little TV before we find ourselves in bed.

This is our routine. We work and live in chaos, managing the best that we can. It wears us down. She will read until her eyes get heavy, and most of the time, I must remove her book from her fingertips, which I kiss so I can feel whole. Most nights, I can doze right off, but not tonight.

My eyes focus on the ceiling.

I hear every single noise. Every single dog bark. Every cat's meow. Every vehicle driving by. Blaring music.

Everything.

But I can hear my heartbeat more than anything else. It becomes louder than the rest, drowning out the animals and the cars. Becoming music to my ears.

I can't sleep. I can't move. I wish for sleep to take me, but it won't. My mind wants something else. It wants to think. It wants to bring doom and gloom. It wants to enter into a world of darkness, a place I don't want to go.

I don't want to live in my nightmares, nor listen to the voice in my head.

But I can't shut it off. I squeeze my eyes together, forcing them closed, straining as hard as I can until my head hurts.

But all I can see is Quentin. All I can think about is him as the worry creeps in.

In foster care, the children in our custody are basically our kids, or that is how it has always been described to me. I've taken it to heart since day one.

Every phone call or text message, I make sure I answer or respond, no matter what time it is.

I can't even count the number of times I've checked my phone since coming home. Looking for an answer. Hoping someone has seen him or that Quentin has decided to return to his foster family.

But there is nothing.

Just that feeling of defeat that has become all too familiar. Like the friend you know will never leave your side.

Not knowing is the worst part when it comes to a runaway. I try not to worry, but that is a losing battle from the get-go, and I know this despite my valiant efforts.

I finally get up and make my way into the kitchen. I grab a glass of water and guzzle it down like I had experienced thirst for days, before going outside and lighting up a smoke from my wife's not-so-secret stash she hid underneath the little table sitting on the balcony.

I take a drag and for a moment, all my worries fade away.

******

"James…"

I feel my body jerk as my eyes shoot open violently. I turn to find Braelynn towering over me. I am covered in sweat. My eyes dart around as I discover that I am outside. I had fallen asleep in my chair.

"Are you okay?" she asks.

I sighing and bury my head in my hands for a few moments, trying to re-enter the world around me. Leaning back and taking a deep breath, I exhale heavily, "I don't know." I want another cigarette so I can let everything fade away once again.

"Your phone has been ringing off the hook, babe. You might want to check it. Maybe they found Quentin. Hell, maybe it's him calling you because he needs help. Knowing him, he probably needs you to bail him out." I say nothing, just stare out at our little city, as if I am searching for him now. "I'll put coffee on," Braelynn says before going back inside.

I don't know how much times passes, but I make my way into the kitchen, guzzle down a cup of coffee before taking a shower and getting dressed. I finish brushing my teeth before turning to find my daughter standing up to my knee with her arms reaching out. I lift her up and press her against my chest. She rests her head on my shoulders and her long, curly hair tickles my face, which results in a smile.

I relish these moments.

They are filled with peace.

But then, that peace is broken by the sound of my phone buzzing. I readjust my daughter in my arms as I walk over and grab my cell. It's my supervisor this time.

"Cindy."

"Where are you?" she fires off, like I don't have thirty-five minutes to get to the office.

"I'm at home. Why?"

There is a sigh followed by a long pause. I can feel my nerves twitching in my skin. Something doesn't feel right, "Cindy? Are you there?"

Another sigh, "They found him, James," and then another pause. I feel my stomach twisting and turning before dropping. "You need to get here as soon as you can."

I don't say anything else. I end the call and let my free arm drop to my side. I suddenly need to sit down, as the room begins to spin. I sit down on the bed, still holding my daughter as close as I can, but right now, there is no peace to be felt.

My phone rings again. This time it is Detective Browning.

"Hello?"

"Good morning…"

I cut him off before he can speak any further, "Where is he?"

I get a location and end the call. I hand my daughter to Braelynn. Grab my keys and I'm out the door without saying a word.

I'm not prepared for this.

I'm not prepared.

I'm not.

3

When I first met Quentin Ross, I wasn't quite sure what to expect. I had my assumptions, which is something they try to beat into your brain when you're going for your bachelor's degree in Social Work. I assumed the absolute worst when I heard about the kid.

I assumed he was going to be an asshole, like most teenagers today. I figured there would be an abundance of arrogance to filter through. Just hearing his name, I was under the assumption that I wasn't going to like him very much.

But then I met him.

Sure, he was cocky at first, but it didn't take long for us to bond. We enjoyed the same music, and I'd even let him listen to the unedited version of the songs. I remember telling him that I couldn't stand listening to music on the radio because of how badly the songs were censored.

I took him shopping, and we joked about how indecisive he was when it came to his apparel. After the first meeting, I felt Quentin was a good kid. I felt that he would be worth fighting for to ensure he had the best possible future.

I never thought his future would turn so grim.

He came from a broken home. Drugs, domestic violence, and all the other key ingredients in fucking up your child's life blended well in the Ross household. Parents were there, but not really. They were there to fight, fuck, and do drugs while Quentin and his siblings had to fend for themselves and learn survival, a mode that Quentin never really escaped from or grew out of.

I know I can relate. The voice in my head, my nightmares, they do not let me forget.

But looking at him now, I wish he had escaped. I wish he would have remained in that mode.

I wish he would have been able to survive whatever hell he had endured before being dumped in an open field west of downtown.

I feel a sickness building up in my stomach, ready to explode from my gut. No matter how many times I close my eyes, I still see him.

The goddamn rope tied around his wrists and ankles. His face nothing more than a mesh of black and purple, dried blood caked over the pale skin that isn't covered in grotesque bruises. It repeats over and over in my head, flashing like when someone takes a picture with a Polaroid. And then the sickness comes. I bury my face in the tall grass a few feet away from the scene. I drop to my hands and knees, hoping to God that I can keep my composure, that I don't lose it. My body feels like it is scrunching up into a tiny ball which I'd be okay with because right now, I don't want the world to see me.

I want to be hidden.

I want to be far away.

I want to fucking die, so I can take Quentin's place. So he can be alive and reach his full potential. To have a better future than he ever imagined.

I don't want to face the truth, because it is so foul and rotten. The truth is a menace, laughing hysterically in my face.

The sickness comes again, as do the tears. My mind floods with another vision. More flashes, filling with more assumptions, but this time, I'm assuming what Quentin went through.

I see him being tortured. I see a group of men, a group of fucking sick puppies beating him, hurting him, having their way with him, as he would plead and beg for them to stop. I see him crying himself to sleep as he curled up into a corner, feeling like he wanted to be hidden, much as I do right now.

Burying my face in my hands, tasting the warmth and the salt of my tears on the tip of my tongue, I question God. I ask where He was, why He didn't protect Quentin.

And then I ask, where was I?

******

Back at the office, Cindy asks me, "Are you okay?"

I don't want to be here right now. I don't want to hear her, either. Wiping tears from my cheeks, I speak in between gasps for air and forgiveness, "I don't know what I am, Cindy. Whatever it is, I know I'm not okay."

"I'm sure this is tough, James."

"Are you, though?"

"What do you mean?"

I feel my blood starting to boil. I am filled with sadness and rage. I want to cry. I want to hurt those who did this to Quentin.

"You didn't see him. You didn't see what had been done to him. His face," tears drop as I grind my teeth and clench my fists, "his fucking face...you could barely tell it was him. Goddamn it!" I shout as I slam my fist down on the arm of my chair, causing Cindy to jump.

She takes a minute to compose herself, taking a deep breath, which is something she tells me to do as well. I don't.

"No, I wasn't there James, but I can tell you're hurt by all of this. That is why I think it would be best for you to take some time off. Clear your head. Get over this and move on as best as you can."

I scoff, "Get over this? Move on? Are you serious right now?"

Cindy sighs as she shakes her head, "James, I am just trying to help you. That is all. I don't have the best solution or anything like that. I'm just trying to go by what I know I'd want if I was in a situation like this."

"It is so easy to just sit here and tell me to clear my head, when you and I both know that I won't be able to clear my head for a very long time. If at all," I say, rising to my feet.

Silence falls between us for a few moments until Cindy sighs once again, "Are you going to take the time off?"

"Yes."

"How much time do you need?"

"I just want to take a leave of absence until I'm ready to come back. Hell, if I even come back at all. After today, I don't know how the fuck I would be able to muster up the strength to come in and sit in my office day after day, trying to help kids day after day without worrying that the same fucking thing is going to happen to them," I state, a numbness creeping in again as my legs start to turn to Jell-O.

I am mad at the world. I am mad at Cindy, because right now in my head, it seems like she is just trying to sugarcoat all this, which only makes things worse. But then, she says something that takes me by surprise, her words filled with a gentleness no one in the office ever really gets to see, "Take as much time as you need. If you need anything, please don't hesitate to ask."

Leaving her office, every move I make, I feel like I'm drowning. I need a drink. One of Braelynn's secret cancer sticks.

Something.

Anything.

Walking toward my office, I see my friend, Darren. He is the only other male in our agency. He is nowhere near as gloomy as me. In fact, I've never seen him upset. We're friends, but it annoys me.

"Hey man, what's up?" He gives a slap on the back, and I hear the voice in my head. I've heard it all morning. It gets louder. "Why the long face, bud?" Darren asks.

"They found one of my foster kids dead this morning. Murdered."

"Oh shit, man," he sighs, "I'm sorry to hear that." He gives me a soft pat on my right shoulder, and I nod, as the voice begins to die down.

"But look at it this way," Darren begins, "that's one less pain in the ass on your caseload, am I right?"

The voice screams. I know what it wants.

I give in, knowing I shouldn't, but Darren has to pay for what he said.

The voice and I agree.

I look at Darren, and I see red.

Then I grab him.

4

"Are you sure you want to do this?" I hear Braelynn ask as I begin packing some of my things into a suitcase. The make and model of the suitcase doesn't matter. Nor does the brand of my shirt, pants, underwear, socks, and shoes. It is all fumes.

I do not take my eyes from my hands as they reach from the dresser over to the suitcase. It all moves in a back-and-forth motion. All I do is speak, my words forming into a statement, "You know that I have to. I've already explained this. I don't want to explain anymore."

She steps closer. I only know this because I hear her footsteps as she shuffles across the floor. I feel a warmth radiating off her. The smell of her perfume almost brings me out of my focused state of mind. I am focused on packing and getting out of this house, going to a place where I need to be. A place where others, at least those that I love and care for, can be safe from any chaos that I can unleash.

I look at her as she stands in the doorway. I let out a sigh, seeing a few tears streaming down her cheeks. She is beautiful, with her sandy blonde hair, her porcelain skin, all the curves in all the right places, light blue eyes that always know how to lure me in. I know this is going to be hard on her. Hell, I tell myself, it's already hard on me. It's been biting at my heart, eating at my soul, taking the very life from me because the woman I see before me has made me feel whole.

"I didn't want it to come to this, babe…" I say, my body feeling as weak as my voice, "But, I can't let anything bad happen. I wouldn't be able to live with myself if anything were to happen… and that I could have prevented it."

I stare into her eyes, knowing that she has never experienced my history of violence. She has her good days and bad days like everyone roaming the Earth, but nothing compared to what I've survived. Braelynn has never known domestic violence or substance abuse. She has never seen how badly those cancers can fuck a life up. I thank God, should He exist, that she has never had to endure what I have. I wouldn't wish that on anyone, even my enemies.

Braelynn is a social worker but should be a model. You'd be blessed to see her in swimsuit magazines and countless others. Working in our chosen field, our paths were destined to line up. When they did, sparks flew. I remember how we started off hot and heavy, meeting up and fucking, spending our days inside as our bodies became entangled in a span of time we never wanted to end. It hasn't, until now.

"I'm not leaving you," I reassure her, "We are still going to be married. I will still think of you and only you." I step closer to her, hoping my words bring her some sort of comfort. "I am doing this for us. You deserve nothing but the best of me. I don't want you to have to live through the ugly of me."

She won't make eye contact, but she takes my hand in hers. "We're married. Through sickness and health, for better or worse," she states before looking up at me. "I agreed to get the best and the worst of you, James. That's why I took your last name. That is why I said yes to becoming an Evans."

The name Evans is synonymous with chaos, at least when it comes to my family tree. I remember when I asked her to marry me, how hesitant I became after she said yes. I couldn't help thinking that her taking my last name would connect her to some sort of curse none of us have ever been able to outrun.

I nod in response. "I know the vows we took. But there are some things from my past, things in my head," I say, pointing to my temple, "I want to protect you from. You're my everything and I don't want to lose that."

She sighs, "But I can't help feeling that I'm losing you."

Before I can say anything, she walks out of the room. Our bedroom. It's already starting to feel like it is no longer ours to share.

When I leave, I know I'll be trading in the king-sized bed as soft as clouds with pillows to match. I'll trade in the overabundance of closet space, filled with name brand clothes and shoes. I will trade in the overpriced windows, leading to a balcony where I can have a bird's-eye view of the city below.

Where I've been the king of the castle on the hill, I will become a resident of a mental health facility. I will wear scrubs. I will sleep on a cot that creaks or snaps with every move I make. The only view of the outside world will be through barred windows. I will be cut off from the world until my doctor, Dr. McIntosh, feels I am okay to re-enter society.

I have tried to prevent this with extra therapy sessions, a change in medication, but there is a voice in my head. He has a name and his name is Abel. He is the worst in me, and he is trying to come out. He wants to cause chaos in my life and in the world around me. In the beginning, Abel was born to be a light in my life, to protect from the darkness I grew up in alongside my siblings. The darkness created by my father. The darkness that consumed my mother, who could not protect me. Could not protect us.

I finish packing and zip my suitcase shut. I lift it off the bed before looking around the room. I begin to tell my things, all my belongings, everything that has fit my personality at some point in my life, goodbye. I tell them that I will see them sooner rather than later. That I hope to do so at least.

I walk through the corridor, looking straight ahead, doing my best to ignore the pictures aligned on each wall. The memories reaching out to me like ghosts in the night trying to grasp for my soul. I reach the living room of my home, glancing into the kitchen as well, and see Braelynn is nowhere to be found.

I call out to her, but there is no answer. I walk into the kitchen to find my medication and a glass of water. I also find a note. I read the note. Braelynn tells me that she didn't have the strength to see me off. That the fact I am leaving, kills her. She tells me that she hopes I get the help that I need and that I don't forget her, because she will not forget me. She tells me that she will be here when I get back. That she loves me.

I fold the letter, placing it in between some of my underwear, as patients are only allowed to bring white T-shirts, underwear, and socks. I let out a sigh before taking my medication and then I walk out of my home, leaving it all behind.

I catch a cab to the airport, taking to the air, making my way to a place I've been countless times before.

New York City.

5

I step outside, searching the surrounding area for Braelynn, despite knowing she is nowhere to be found. I hear a sound, the clearing of a throat, coming from behind me. I turn to find Abel standing there. He looks like me. Our skin slightly tan. Our light brown hair, our muscular jawline, our dark blue eyes. The only difference happens to be the scars riddling his face.

The city welcomes us. The skies are grey, sort of matching my mood. I look around at the various buildings and skyscrapers that are known to litter the city of New York. It is its own little world. The occupants, including myself, offer a whole cast of characters, each in their own little universe, living a different variation of what could be deemed a normal existence.

I hail a cab and climb inside. Abel follows. The Evans family curse knows no bounds. Nothing can stop the sickness. Not even a good dose of this or that medication. What the doctor orders doesn't know how to kill this sickness. I often question whether I was born with it, or if it was forced into my life, a plague within my DNA.

Abel and I sit in silence as the cab carries us through the city. He looks out one window as I gaze out the other. He counts how many homeless people he sees. We feel bad for them, but he also snickers at them. The part of me that feels no sympathy.

The cab reaches its destination. A train station. I check in before taking a seat, waiting for my train to be called. Abel takes a seat beside me. I look around, noticing that I've sat as far away from the rest of the traveling world as I possibly can. Abel leans in close, and he speaks, his voice raspy, "We need to talk."

Still scanning the room, I say, "There's nothing to discuss."

"Of course, there is," he replies. "You know damn well that there is plenty to talk about, James."

Not looking at him, I say, "I'm not talking about it. Nothing you say is going to change the decision I've made."

Abel grunts and shakes his head. I see this out of the corner of my eye. I keep an eye on him out of habit. To make sure he's not slipped into the driver's seat. To make sure he's not about to do something that could land me in prison. My history of violence flows through him like the blood in my veins. He feeds on it like cancer feeds on life.

I remember when he first came back and how he told me how much he had changed, because I had changed since our last journey together. Thinking of it now, I can't help but think of that old phrase, stating that the more things change, the more they stay the same.

My train is called and I… we… walk among the rest of the world, all scurrying along like worker ants living their everyday normal lives, with their everyday normal problems. I have craved that for so long that the very thought of living an everyday normal life scares the absolute shit out of me.

I reach my cabin and Abel steps inside with me. I close the door, as I requested a private cabin, figuring that Abel would force his way into a debate with me. As soon as the door closes, he speaks, letting me know that I was right.

"You don't need to do this."

"Yes, I do, Abel. Things haven't gotten any better since you've returned. I'm already becoming more violent. I am not going to allow things to go too far," I say as my eyes rest upon the outside world as it slowly begins to slip away.

"Things will never be perfect, James," he calmly states. "You need to realize that you have rage inside of you. You have suppressed it for so long with this nice guy routine, that you've only made things worse. I am trying to help you get it out. I'm trying to help you find and maintain balance."

I turn, glaring at him, and my hands go to work as they open my bag and reach inside. I draw my hand back out, my fingers clasping my medications as I keep my eyes locked with his. "These…" I say, shaking the bottles, "These give me balance. These help me maintain. Your presence is an insult to what these do."

Abel chuckles as he shakes his head. "You really believe that?"

"I don't know what to believe," I reply.

He leans over, grazing one of the bottles with his fingertips. "If these were working, I wouldn't be here, James. You would be completely numb to everything. There would be no violence, just as you wouldn't really have any happiness."

I cut him off. "Is this the part where you tell me that happiness cannot exist without violence, Abel? That it's like good and evil?"

Abel shakes his head once more. "No, because you already know that. You don't need me to tell you."

I go to respond but I swallow my words as well as my pride, knowing deep down that Abel is right. Light doesn't exist without darkness. Good doesn't exist without evil. Happiness can't exist without violence or sadness. They need each other to maintain balance.

But I ask myself, does that mean I need Abel to remain balanced?

The thought crosses my mind over and over on some sort of loop as our eyes remain locked. He knows what I'm thinking. I can tell this to be true based on the smirk painted all over his scarred face.

I also tell myself these are excellent questions to bring up in therapy. I place my meds back in the back, replacing them with my journal and a pen. I open to a blank page, writing down the questions to ask.

"Do you really think you're going to get an honest answer to any of this?"

Abel's question resonates in my ear, but I fight the urge to respond. I don't want to give him the fucking satisfaction. I glance at Abel before slamming the journal shut and dropping it back in my bag, returning my focus to the world as we pass it by, hoping to get lost in the nonexistent beauty of the city. To get lost in anything other than my head, where Abel lives and breathes.

I grow tired but I fight my body's longing for sleep, telling myself that Abel can go and do as he pleases if I sleep. The last thing I need is to sleep only to wake up in a jail cell because he decided to pick a fight with someone. He almost hurt a friend of mine a week or so ago due to an argument. My friend, as I know deep down, wants the best for me, but Abel wasn't having that. I know Abel thinks he is the best for me.

Here I go again, I tell myself, getting lost in my head. I zone in on the buildings, big and small, as the train zooms past them. The buildings are soon replaced with trees and infinite wilderness, where everything lives under the law of the jungle. I tell myself that law exists well outside the jungle. It is alive and well in all aspects of life.

Stepping off the train with Abel in tow, I find myself greeted by someone named Maxwell. "Hello. James Evans?" he asks, extending a hand, which I shake. "I'm Maxwell. I'm here to pick you up."

I stare at him, confusion popping out of my eyes. "Yes, I'm James Evans. Why are you picking me up and where would you be taking me?"

"I've been sent by Dr. McIntosh," he states as if I should already know this. "I'm here to transport you to the facility."

I nod. "I'm sorry. I'm not against you picking me up. It's just that I've gone to this facility before and I've never had a driver. It's just unusual. That's all."

"Well," Maxwell begins, his green eyes staring at me through dark brown hair ruffled by his hat, "Dr. McIntosh has instructed me to take very good care of you, since you are a very special client. I guess being an athlete has its perks, right?"

"Yeah, I guess so."

Before anything else can be said, Maxwell grabs my bag from my hand and turns away, heading off in the opposite direction. I look at Abel, who looks back at me. There is a slight hint of dread on his face, but I tell myself that dread stems from the fact of where I'm going. I'm going to a place that will help me get rid of him.

"Hey, I'm sorry if I came off like a dick," I say as I catch up to Maxwell as we exit the train station. He doesn't say anything. Maxwell continues walking, leading Abel and I toward a limo. "McIntosh told you to pick me up in a limo?"

Maxwell throws my bag in the backseat before looking at me. The look in his eyes gives away the fact he is annoyed by my question, possibly my presence, period. "I guess he wants his special patient riding in style on the way to a psych hospital," he shrugs. "I don't know which is crazier." He opens the passenger door. I climb inside, as does Abel, and I look at Maxwell just before he closes the door. "Enjoy the trip."

6

I look around the limo, telling myself that I can get comfortable. That everything is fine. That it really isn't unusual to be driven in a limo on my way to a mental health facility. But I can't get over the fact there is a part of me that agrees with Maxwell. I don't which is crazier, being considered a special patient or riding in a limo to a place that has been built to house people like me, with insanity echoing within.

The window separating Maxwell and me draws down, and he stares at me from the driver's seat. "Do you want the window up or down?"

My eyes glance over at Abel, knowing that he's craving conversation, before looking back at Maxwell. "You can leave it up."

Maxwell nods. "Suit yourself. If you need anything just buzz me," he states, motioning with his head to a button to the right of me. The window rolls up and once again I'm alone with Abel.

"I don't like this," he calls out.

I shake my head, "And I don't care, Abel. I'm not sure if you've realized that yet. Just as I'm not sure if you've realized that this is happening whether you like it or not. This isn't about you. It's about me."

Abel scoffs, "And you call me selfish."

"No, I believe I've called you a monster," I fire back.

"Just remember," Abel leans forward, pointing a finger at me, "That I was born from all the bad things you've kept inside. That is what makes me the monster you've claimed me to be."

I close my eyes and shake my head. "Please... just please... shut the hell up, Abel." I sigh before I dig into my bag, grabbing my journal as well as the pen. I begin writing under the list of questions from earlier, telling myself to be sure to get rid of the bad things I've kept inside.

"This doesn't look familiar," I hear Abel say, which snaps my attention from my writing.

I look outside. The view is different from the last time I drove to the facility. "No, it doesn't," I respond before looking at Abel. "Maybe he's taking a different route. Avoiding road work of some kind."

Abel groans, "Don't give me that shit. I know you don't trust him, because I don't trust him."

"Fine," I say, "I'll ask Maxwell." I press the button beside me on the door. A slight buzzing sound fills the limo.

Maxwell's voice blares through a little intercom, "Yes, sir? What can I do for you?"

"I noticed we're on a different route than I've taken before," I say, feeling a slight dread like what was on Abel's face before we left the station. I recall Abel taking the trip with me the first time I went to the facility. He was as unhappy as he is now. "I wanted to know if everything was alright, or if there's anything that I need to be aware of."

There is a slight pause between Maxwell and me. I buzz him again before he finally replies, "Everything is under control, sir," and then, communication dies.

"I told you that I didn't like this," Abel reminds me.

I tell myself that he is freaking out because despite the calm demeanor I usually carry when things are going ape shit in my head, I am freaking out as well. I take a few deep breaths, telling myself that everything is okay.

Everything is okay.

Everything is okay.

Everything is...

I press the button to buzz Maxwell once again, but nothing happens. There is no sound. I fumble through my bag, searching for my cell. Maybe I can call Braelynn to tell her what is going on. That thought runs through my mind as I check for bars. That thought dies quickly as I realize I have no service.

I try it again.

Everything is okay.

Everything is okay.

"Stop it!" Abel shouts at me, causing the panic to surface a little more. "I don't know about you but everything about this situation screams that it is completely fucked. Which means you and I are in that same boat."

I take another deep breath. I check for cell service again, but still nothing. Questions begin to fill my head. Why did I get into the car? Why didn't I trust myself when I felt it was unusual? Would McIntosh put me in a dangerous situation? If he would, why?

No, no, no.

I tell myself that I can trust McIntosh. That he is a good doctor. That he wants what is best for me.

Trust him? Can't I? He is a good doctor, isn't he? He does want what is best for me, right?

I look over at Abel, but he isn't there. Panic rises a bit more than I understand that now I'm all alone, not knowing a damn thing about where I'm heading or what will happen when the limo reaches its destination.

I take a few more deep breaths. The song of "Everything is Okay" is on repeat in my head. My breathing slows. I start to feel a sense of calm.

Then, the limo stops.

7

I feel my heart pounding against my chest. My muscles tense up as my mind and body prepare for the worst. I hear a door opening and closing, followed by the crunch, crunch, crunch, of footsteps drawing near.

Then, the door opens.

I look out to find Maxwell and another man wearing nursing scrubs, staring at me through black-framed glasses and perfectly kept salty hair. Behind them stands a building I've never seen nor heard of before.

The scrubs with the glasses finally speaks. "You must be James." He holds out his hand as I hang half in and out of the limo. "I'm Jeffrey. Welcome to the Trinity Institute."

I take his hand, hesitantly shaking it before climbing out of the car. I look at what Jeffrey called the Trinity Institute. I see six buildings, spaced out in a triangular pattern. The marble sign welcomes anyone and everyone to Trinity. The sign has flowers intertwining with the letters, making it seem wholesome. I know Abel will disagree.

"Why am I here and not the Vaughn Institute?" I ask, referring to the facility I stayed during my last battle with Abel that was supposed to cure me, but clearly did not.

"Were you not told you'd be coming here?" Jeffrey asks, looking shocked and confused by my question.

Shaking my head, I say, "No. I wasn't told anything of the sort. I was led to believe I'd be going to Vaughn." I then turn my attention to Maxwell, "I asked your driver here where he was taking me, but he didn't tell me shit. I don't appreciate that one fucking bit."

Jeffrey shoots Maxwell a look who throws his hands up in surrender, "I thought he heard me. Mr. Evans buzzed me, asking where we were headed. I told him. I thought he heard me. I do apologize. It must have been an equipment malfunction in the limo."

"An equipment malfunction?" I feel myself growing agitated. I take a deep breath, knowing an appearance from Abel would not be the best course of action.

Jeffrey steps in, "Maxwell, you should have known to make sure Mr. Evans knew where he was headed before he even stepped foot inside the vehicle. I will be sure to report this to Dr. McIntosh. He will alert your employer who is contracted with us." Jeffrey then turns to me, "Mr. Evans, I know you were unaware of a lot in this situation and for that, I do apologize. However, you're here now. Do you still want to go through with this?"

I look at Maxwell, who stares down at the ground, shaking his head and cursing anyone and everyone. I think about going back to Braelynn, back to my life, wondering if I can manage, but the very thought causes me to sigh and shake my head. I don't think I can do it. "Jeffrey, I'm still here."

Jeffrey smiles from ear to ear before getting my bag out of the car. He extends his arm and takes a bow. "Right this way, sir."

He leads the way and I follow. Despite the bullshit with Maxwell, being around Jeffrey brings back that sense of calm I had momentarily in the limo. "So, tell me about this place, Jeffrey," I say as we edge closer to what appears to be the main entrance to the facility.

"It is a place of vision," Jeffrey states before opening the front door and letting me step inside. "Right from the mind of Dr. McIntosh. He didn't like the way things were done at the Vaughn Institute, so he set out to fight the wars of mental health his own way. He renovated this place, which was an abandoned facility for the mentally ill and criminally insane," he says, practically beaming.

The thought of being around the criminally insane makes my stomach churn. Jeffrey continues, "Heck, from what I've learned from other staff members, and even Dr. McIntosh himself, the grounds are said to be haunted."

"Haunted?"

Jeffrey nods, "Oh yes, by the spirits of some patients who died here long ago. They say they were buried on the grounds. There have been stories where patients and staff have seen shadows on the walls, just people walking back and forth, but when you look down the halls, no one is there. Just what you see on the walls."

I shake my head, "I'm not much for superstition, Jeffrey."

He shrugs his broad shoulders, "Well, the way I see it," he says, opening another door for me, "none of us would be in a place like this if we weren't a little superstitious."

I step through the door where I am welcomed by a busy beehive of nursing staff. Bright lights. Walls like skyscrapers. Everything looks comforting. Everything is serene. I look at Jeffrey as he steps beside me, "Ghosts haunt this place? It looks like a paradise. There's no way."

"Hey, Mr. Evans, I'm not saying I've seen anything in terms of ghosts. I'm only telling you what I've heard."

"This doesn't look like any mental health facility I've ever seen," I state, looking around, trying to take it all in.

He nods. "Dr. McIntosh didn't want it to give off that sense of dread most places like this have. He wanted it to be welcoming. He felt if it intimidated the patients then no work could really be done. He felt the patients would keep themselves closed off, therefore never really improving."

I nod. "I have to admit," I begin, "I've been very apprehensive about working with McIntosh after meeting him a few months ago, but hearing you say that," I turn to Jeffrey, "it definitely restores my faith in the man."

Jeffrey gleams. "I'm glad I could be of help. Here is your bag, Mr. Evans. Let's get you signed in. While you're doing that, I will make sure your room is ready. Pleasure to meet you, Mr. Evans. I will be with you before you know it."

He points me in the direction of the front desk. I walk over, finding myself talking to a rather attractive brunette. She flashes me a seductive look before handing me paperwork. I take a seat in a chair which sinks in and feels like I'm on clouds, reminding me of home. Reminding me of the bed I share with my wife. I remember Braelynn, but I shake those thoughts, those memories, away as I remind myself of why I'm here.

To better myself.

For her and everyone else I care about.

8

I go to work on the tedious and repetitive forms. Going over my list of issues, despite the feeling I'm doing the right thing, depresses me some. I remind myself of my purpose for being here. As I am filling them out, the feeling of joy returns, and rises within me. I tell myself that this is why I've not heard from Abel since I arrived. He cannot stand any sort of happiness or positivity.

Once I'm finished with the paperwork, I return to the reception desk. The brunette looks at me before reading through the forms, nodding with each flip of a page. She then turns to me and says, "Hand over your cell phone, wallet, and any other personal belongings of yours." She reaches down below, her hands re-emerging with a plastic tote. "Place all belongings in here."

I stare at her, finding myself in a joking mood. "Wait, what? You want my cell? My wallet? What about my bag? I'm going to need my stuff."

She shakes her head, clearly nowhere near being jovial, "Mr. Evans, your cell will be a distraction from the work we are trying to do here. In order to improve who you are, you will need no distractions. As for the contents of your bag, we will search through it and will return what we deem necessary to you before the end of the day."

I stare at her, trying to get a read, but to no avail. The brunette stands firm in her position. I remind myself of the feeling I had of joy and comfort. I decide to get it back, so I hand over my belongings, giving away my contact to the outside world, all for McIntosh's vision for me to better myself.

I settle into my room. Everything is white. From the walls to the ceiling, it is a sea of white. Very bland. Very plain. Except for a desk that sits in the far corner from my bed, complete with a pillow covered in a white pillowcase and white sheets. The room temperature isn't too hot or too cold. It feels just right.

Compared to the Vaughn Institute, this truly is a luxury. Mental patients living the high life. An orderly arrives, handing me a pair of scrubs. He tells me to strip down to my underwear. I stand there waiting for him to leave, but he doesn't. My experience here may be all about comfort, but it seems it's hard to miss those awkward moments.

I slip into the scrubs, picking up my shirt, blue jeans, and boots before handing them to the orderly, "Thanks," I say, but I get no verbal response. Just a long stare. Like all of time and space has stopped moving, as if we are stuck in a never-ending continuum where we must stare at one another until oblivion claims us both.

Oblivion doesn't come. He grunts before slowly backing out of my room. Releasing a sigh, I take a seat on the edge of the bed. My eyes zone in on the floor as I sit and twiddle my thumbs. It reminds me of my grandfather.

He would always twiddle his thumbs. I always thought he did it due to being nervous, but I learned, as I got older, that he did it out of boredom. I never quite grew out of doing it due to nervousness. Sitting in silence makes me nervous, always has. Maybe it will cease once I return home.

Memories of home start to flood my mind, but Abel speaks, bringing me back to the room. "Don't think about home," he says as he strolls around the room.

"It's hard not to," I reply, returning my eyes to the floor, my thumbs still rotating around each other in a circular motion.

"We don't need to be here," Abel states. "I can't believe you don't see that."

My thumbs begin rotating faster, "You're so fucking persistent, Abel. I can't believe you still can't see just how much your opinion doesn't matter. Especially at this point."

"You're going to need me in order to survive this, James. You're being stupid right now!" Abel shouts. He shakes his head. "I don't know what I have to do in order for you to get it through your fucking head."

"My fucking head?!" I repeat his statement with a slight chuckle. "My head? Do you care to repeat that, Abel?" I look up at him, "You said it best. It is my head." I press a finger to the center of my forehead, "My head, not yours. You belong in here, only because what is in here created you."

"You're being fucking ridiculous."

I almost respond before the door to my room to flies open. I no longer see Abel. I only see Dr. McIntosh as he enters.

"How are you, James?"

I shrug. "I could be better. You know, well enough to where I don't need to be in a place like this."

McIntosh, with his black, slowly fading into silver hair rising to a tip in the middle of the top of his head, and a beard that looks like ashes from a dying fire, frowns. "I understand, James but remember there is nothing wrong with seeking help for your mental health. If more people did that, then the world may not be as chaotic as it is now. We may not have to worry with shootings or bombings, at least not at the rate we've seen over the last few years."

"I guess you could say that's why I'm here," I reply, my thumbs slowly coming to a halt. "I want to avoid going down that route myself."

"Do you feel you would become so enraged that you would cause acts of violence, James?"

The question sends a shock wave through my brain. Memories of previous violence begin ricocheting back and forth in my mind. My fingers clenched into fists.

"James?"

My hands slowly relax as I lock eyes with McIntosh. "Yes?"

"Is that a yes to my question or are you asking 'yes'?"

"I got lost in thought, Doc. I'm sorry."

He sighs. "It's alright. Now, do you care to answer my question? Do you think you're capable of acts of violence?"

Being able to tell people what they want to hear is a trick one learns very quickly when coming from a broken home or having experienced trauma on any and all levels. I sigh as well, remembering how I have told so many therapists throughout my life that I feel better. That nothing is any longer bothering me. Each therapist received a new lie. Running from the truth never helped me in the past, I tell myself. Running from it isn't going to help me now.

"I don't really know what I'm capable of, Doc. In regard to the ugly inside me, I'm here to get rid of it. I want to rip it out and bury it so that it'll never surface again. So that the ugly inside me can stay dead. I mean, as I read in a book somewhere," I clear my throat, "dead is better."

McIntosh laughs. "I've seen that. But in a movie, not a book. Reading things like that," he says with a shake of the head, "not my style."

I snicker, "I understand. So, what do we do now, Doc? I'm here. Do I sit here the rest of the day, or…?"

"Ah," he replies, "You want to know the day-to-day process here at Trinity?"

"Beats twiddling my thumbs."

"Well, we typically have a group therapy either in the morning or at noon. We have three meals a day, of course. Some patients get to participate in recreational activities depending on their mental status. For example, you could go work out, as we have a weight room here on the grounds. You like to stay in shape, as I recall."

"That I do."

"When patients first arrive, we have to put them through a separate process. You've given up your belongings and are in the attire we've deemed appropriate. There is one final piece," he states.

Still seated on the edge of the bed I ask, "And what might that be?"

McIntosh smirks, "My colleagues and I believe it is necessary, while patients feel it's evil. I guess that would mean it is a necessary evil."

Cocking an eyebrow, I stare at him, feeling jumbled. "So, what you're saying is that I'm not going to like it."

McIntosh shakes his head, "Most certainly not. But as I stated, it's a necessary portion of the process. Before we can move forward, we need to have you do this one last thing. Are you ready?"

"With the way you're describing things, Doc," I retort, "seems like I don't have much of a choice in the matter."

He shrugs his shoulders, "Well, you can leave any time you want, James, but you've already said you're not sure what you're capable of. That is why you're here. If I understand you correctly, leaving wouldn't be doing you any good."

"What do I have to do?"

He motions with his finger. "Follow me."

9

I follow him and he leads me to a barber's chair. I look at the chair then at him. "What is this? Am I going off to war?"

McIntosh shrugs as a bald man wearing a white apron steps into the room. I watch as he walks over to a dresser before the buzzing sound of clippers enters my ears. I look back at McIntosh as he says, "You may not be picking up a gun and going overseas to fight, but from what I've read of your file, you're in your own little war, James."

"I still don't get why you want me to have my head shaved, Doc. It's strange. More than a little if you ask me," I reply.

He shrugs once more, "Every patient you will see and meet," he begins, adjusting his glasses in the process, "their heads are shaved as well. I have done this to create a sense of equality here. Everyone that walks through the front door... they arrive with their own brand of issues. Each set of issues are different from those of another patient. A patient typically feels that he or she is the only person suffering from what they are dealing with. I am here to let them know that no matter what they are going through, they are still human. Like the rest of us."

I take his words into consideration. I recall my teenage years, where I felt that the hell my siblings and I were going through was only ours. That no one else had to endure it. I remember when Abel first arrived and how I felt that I was the only person walking this Earth that had a voice inside of his head. I recall how often I still feel that way.

"Remember," McIntosh says, breaking me from thought, "you can leave at any time, James. You don't have to have your head shaved. You don't have to do any of this. It is your choice."

I sigh, "You really drive a hard bargain, Doc." I nod to the barber before taking a seat. He spins me around and drapes an apron over me, tying the strings gently around my neck. I look at McIntosh and say, "I like the idea of feeling equal. I can remember quite a bit, but I can honestly say that I don't recall the last time I felt that. Like I was a part of something."

McIntosh nods. "Then consider this your home away from home. I want you, as well as my other patients, to see this place not as a mental health facility. I want you all to see it as your own personal wonderland."

Hearing the term 'wonderland' causes me to go quiet. I don't utter another word as the barber goes to work on my hair. Strand upon strand falls to the floor below, forming clump after clump. McIntosh stands in the doorway to the room, watching. I know going down the rabbit hole never ends well. The entire idea behind him presenting Trinity to the patients as such bothers me in ways I can't describe.

I sigh as the hair keeps falling, telling myself to keep an open mind. That everything will be okay. That I have no reason to think otherwise.

"You're all done," I hear the barber say before he spins me around to where I see my reflection in the mirror at his station, "What do you think?"

"It's different," I say, running a hand over my head. I glance over at McIntosh. "Now what?"

"Now, we go to therapy."

He motions for me to follow once again and I do. We go down several corridors. "This place feels like a maze. I'd be surprised if people haven't gotten lost in here."

McIntosh laughs, "In a way, it is. We are all still trying to figure it out."

"So, are we only in this building?"

"How do you mean?"

I reply, "There are several buildings, but so far it only seems like this one is in use."

He shakes his head, "No. The other buildings are like dorms. Each building houses patients based on the needed level of care. The building in the very back houses the most violent of our patients."

His response makes me feel uneasy. "How violent are we talking, Doc?"

Clearing his throat, McIntosh replies, "The patients consist of murderers and rapists. Very violent people who have committed very violent crimes. They are brought here based on court order. We try to rehabilitate them."

I stop in my tracks. McIntosh does the same and spins around, facing me. "You want to rehabilitate them?" I say incredulously. "How is that even possible?"

"I'm not saying that it is," he begins, "but I'm still going to try. I'm not saying that they will be released back into society, because you can take a man out of the wild, but you cannot take the wild out of him. We would work with them, helping them with their own histories of violence, and then they would stay here in the community I've built. They would be able to stay in a building such as this. Does that make sense?"

"I've got to admit that it doesn't make sense. You're talking about rehabilitating someone who has taken a life. Or many lives. On purpose or for the fun of it. I don't see a change being made. I'm surprised they're here instead of prison."

McIntosh nods. "I understand your point, but you see, the courts believe in what I'm doing, or at least attempting to do. So many things can be done with one's mind, James. Take yours for example. You've committed acts of violence or hallucinated that you've committed acts of violence. You are here seeking help and I wouldn't let you leave until I felt you were no longer a potential danger to yourself."

His statement shakes me somewhat. "What do you mean you wouldn't let me leave? I thought you said that I could leave whenever I wanted?"

"Did I?"

"Yes, you did," I say matter-of-factly.

Silence falls between us for a few moments. McIntosh looks at me then down at the floor, as if he is trying to hide the fact that he's made a terrible mistake. Then, he laughs.

"What's so funny?" I ask, not finding the situation humorous in the slightest.

He shakes his head, "I'm only fooling with you, James. You can leave whenever you want. But, the men and women in the building I just spoke of, they cannot leave unless I am able to provide enough evidence to say it would be okay."

"Are you sure you're only messing with me?"

He nods his head once again. "Oh yes, absolutely. I'm not the sort of person to hold someone against their own free will, James. I'm not some sort of monster."

I give a slight nod before our journey picks up where we left off. I am led to another room, where several other patients, all with their heads shaved, are seated in a circle.

McIntosh greets them, "Good afternoon, everyone. I'd like to introduce you all to our newest member. His name is James. Say hello, James."

I give a weak wave before joining the circle. I look at McIntosh off and on, wondering if he really was joking around, because for someone who doesn't seem like the type to make a mistake, his eyes told me he was backtracking.

I sigh, telling myself it's all in my head.

10

I observe the therapy session. Everyone takes a turn, telling McIntosh and the rest of us how they are doing, or feeling. Each person stressing their issues and how they hope to get better so they can return home to those they left behind. Hearing their stories causes me to think of Braelynn, and Sophie.

I curse myself for just now thinking of her. Sophie and I have developed quite the relationship since I left Vaughn. I think about our bond over comic books and all things superhero.

Before any other thoughts of her can cross my mind, I hear my name. I turn to see McIntosh as well as the other patients all staring at me. I ask, "Yes?"

He replies, "Would you like to share with us today, James?"

I tell myself that there is so much that I could share. I could share about how I've recently attacked co-workers as well as friends. I could share how Abel is the voice behind all my anger. I could share so much, but instead I shake my head, "No. Not today."

He nods. "I see," he says, looking concerned. "Just know this, James. This is a safe place. There are no judgments here. Are there?" he asks, looking around at the rest of the circle. All of them shake their heads from side to side before McIntosh continues, "You cannot work through any of your issues if you don't talk about them. You have to let them come up for air, James, so that you, along with the rest of us, can see them exposed."

I tighten my jaw, crossing my arms over my chest, not enjoying the feeling I'm getting of being lectured. I nod. "I'll talk when I'm ready."

McIntosh sighs once again. "Fair enough." He then looks to the person beside me. "Would you like to share?"

Everything continues without me truly participating. We then break for dinner. I eat alone, which is fine. I am still a little irked with what McIntosh had said about me being able to leave. This conjures up memories of Maxwell and the weird drive. Meeting Jeffrey brought comfort. I tell myself that I should seek him out because he was able to keep me level-headed before, but instead I just sit in silence, stuffing my face with a nicely prepared three course meal that one wouldn't normally expect from a mental health facility.

Trinity, I tell myself, is anything but normal.

After dinner, it is meds. It's like you see in the movies. We all get in line, waiting our turn to get pills and a paper cup filled with water. They check our tongues to ensure we've swallowed. Once meds are finished, we are told to return to our rooms for lights out. I head down the hallway, walking among other patients before one of them reaches over and grabs my arm. I feel Abel trying to take over almost instantly.

I jerk my arm away, glaring at this dark-haired fellow, greasy from head to toe. "What the hell?!"

He puts his hands up, yielding. "I come in peace, James. I'm sorry to have startled you."

The tension coursing through my body slowly fades. I can feel Abel stepping back. I nod. "You can put your hands down. I'm sorry that I overreacted," a verbal throwback to my days in anger management.

He shakes his head, "No, it's all good, brother. I understand. New place, new face. It's hard not to be on edge if you ask me."

"Well," I say, sticking out my hand, "you know my name. What's yours?"

His hand embraces mine. "The name's Lance. Pleasure to meet you."

"Likewise."

He looks down both ends of the hallway before staring back at me. "Just wanted to tell you to not let this place get you down. McIntosh, either. You talk when you're ready, like you said."

"I have my doubts about this place," I say as we stand in the middle of the hallway, patients still walking by us, "but I'm trying to tell myself it's all in my head."

Lance nods, "That's probably the best advice. Just remember why you're here."

"Will do," I say before we head off in opposite directions. I enter my room. I still have a little residue of adrenaline running through me so I do some push-ups and sit-ups until the muscles light up like there's a fire inside before my body grows tired.

I lie down, pulling the sheet over me. I tell myself that today was a rough day but that things will get better, trying to be optimistic. First days are always rough, I tell myself with a slight scoff.

Tomorrow will be better.

Then the door to my room opens. I watch as Jeffrey steps into the room, closing the door behind him. I ask him if he needs anything but there is no answer as he slowly creeps toward me. I tell myself that day one doesn't seem to over. I tell myself that day one may be getting a lot worse.

11

I walk through a room. It is all white. I'm wearing a black suit and tie. I see my wife. I see my daughter. They are standing at the end of what appears to be a row of rooms. The doors to each room stand wide open as I travel toward the end.

Each room is a different color. One is black, the next one is green. I do my best to keep my eyes on Braelynn and Sophie. Sophie with her jet-black hair, her eyes blue like mine. I can see her smile as she looks up at my wife. I get a little closer and I can see they are in a kitchen. It isn't the one from the home I share with Braelynn.

They are laughing and giggling. Braelynn holds a green plastic bowl. Lime green, like the walls surrounding them. She is stirring something with a wooden spoon. Sophie appears to be rolling dough. They are both wearing white T-shirts with red and green aprons. I can't help but chuckle at the happiness that I can't wait to be a part of.

I step through another room, and then I suddenly stop. A loud crashing sound erupts behind me. I turn to see all the doors I've walked by begin slamming closed. The doors start to slam harder and faster. I try to reach my family, racing through the remaining rooms. As I get closer, however, the rooms ahead of me commence in crumbling. The snapping and cracking sounds echo in my ears, growing louder by the second.

Debris begins falling all around me, hitting my arms, just as the floor below starts coming apart. I jump from side to side as the floor and ceiling I race around divides in every which way, and then I reach the last room. The destruction stops.

I am separated from my family by nothing more than air, as if we are drifting through space.

I reach out. "Braelynn... Sophie..."

They stop simultaneously before stepping out of the kitchen and into the doorway. They look at me as if they don't see me. They look at me, their eyes soulless. Their eyes become completely black. I call out to them again, but I get nothing.

"Sophie, sweetie. It's Dad. Can you help me get over to you and Braelynn?"

She remains silent.

"Braelynn," I say as I brace myself against the door frame, "can you help me?" She remains silent as well. I slowly reach over, trying to keep my balance, and to avoid looking down at the abyss below. I grab hold of their door frame as I take a few deep breaths before leaping across into their room. I try speaking to them, but silent they remain. I finally reach out, placing my hand on my wife's shoulder. Their skin grows pale as Braelynn's mouth opens and she releases a scream, the sound of which I've never heard before. Blood begins to drip from their eyes as Sophie begins screaming as well.

Their screams cause a chain reaction. The remaining rooms begin falling apart and then the floor beneath slowly opens. I fall, trying my best to grasp for them, for anything that I can get my hands on, but I find nothing. Just space. As I fall, I look up at them and they stare down at me. Their screams become silence.

And then, I wake up.

12

I blink as the world comes to me. I'm no longer floating in a void. Just four white walls, like I am some sort of figurine being sent via mail, in a boxed package. My head throbs and I try to sit up in my bed, but pain courses through my body, shooting from my head to my toes.

There is no sound except for the ringing in my ears. Each time I try to move, the ringing transforms into the sound of rocks being ground together. I rest my head against the pillow, telling myself to give it a few minutes. And then I ask why my head is throbbing the way that it is. Did I fall yesterday?

Did I hit my head? I press the back of my skull deeper into the pillow as I try to remember what happened yesterday. I remember talking with Braelynn before I left our house. I also recall the bickering with Abel as we made our way to the train station, on the train, and even after we met Maxwell.

I recollect the journey with Maxwell and how it quickly became a nightmare. I see myself in quite the panic, bouncing back and forth in the back of the limousine. I see Jeffrey greeting me, giving some comfort, ensuring me the nightmare had ended. I remember walking into Trinity and all the views I had seen before handing all of my belongings to reception.

I remember being led to my room and giving my clothes over as well. I remember the conversation with McIntosh before having my head shaved. I run a hand over my head just to check. My hair is still gone.

I remember only fragments after that. I remember being in a group session, but I can't recall anything that was said. I try to remember if there was anything that McIntosh and I had talked about before meeting with the group, but nothing comes. I see fragments, images of standing across from him, as well as meeting Max, but it becomes a puzzle that I simply can't piece together.

I close my eyes and whisper, "Abel? Are you there?"

I wait for an answer that never comes. It reminds me of several times growing up, asking for a parent that would never come. I remember having to go to them, finding my mother with a syringe resting in her hand as her eyes and face were glazed over. I remember finding my father doing lines of coke in the basement, sitting in the dark. I remember, after entering each room, calling out to them, only for my mother and father to look back at me vacuously.

I see them now, staring at me as if I don't exist. I know, to them, I never did unless it was convenient.

I call out to Abel once more, but still nothing. I slowly rise in my bed. My bones popping while the gravel grinds once again in my head. I lean over, still trying to piece the fragments together, failing miserably in the process.

I stare down at the floor, doing my best to keep myself held up as all the miserable feelings rise from my stomach, burning my throat and tongue before becoming an artful masterpiece of the floor. I grow weak as my arms give out. I fall face first into my own thick sickness. I lift my head, calling out for help, hoping that someone saves me from drowning in my own vomit.

I turn my head to the side as the gravel grinding escalates. I open my mouth, begging for help, feeling paralyzed all over. I search for an orderly, a doctor, a god, asking why this is happening to me, until I see Abel standing at the opposite end of the room. He stands in the corner, but he doesn't make eye contact. He looks down and shakes his head. I watch him do this until a group of scrubs rush into my room to save my life.

13

The scrubs vanish eventually. My room becomes the cafeteria. More white walls, but on a much larger scale. The patients sit at the finest of dining room tables, like something you'd see in a castle during Medieval times. They all seem happy and content, stuffing their faces with a gourmet breakfast, while I'm trying to figure out when and how I made it in here.

I drive my fork into my eggs, scrambled like the thoughts in my head. I'm still trying to piece everything together, because I still can't remember what happened after the last therapy session from the night before. I barely remember this morning. Everything is fragmented. Trying to force the memories to come to life causes my head to hurt again.

I can't help but feel like someone has taken a screwdriver to my temporal lobe, broken into my mind, and rearranged the filing cabinet I have in my head. Like a thief struck in the night, digging through the files that contain all my memories, and they decided that it would be a good idea to fuck with what happened to me yesterday. But I ask myself as I take a bite of my eggs and try to make it seem like I am not on the verge of a nervous breakdown, why would they want to mess with only yesterday?

Nothing happened, right? I ask myself as if I expect an answer. I remind myself that Abel didn't speak to me earlier this morning. He only watched me as the sickness left my body.

Where are you, Abel? You were all talk when we were in the limo, but now you barely show your face? Especially when I actually need you? How ironic, I think to myself as I take a sip of my coffee. As I place my coffee mug down, I see Jeffrey walk in. I give him a wave, but he looks right through me. Am I one of the ghosts he mentioned when I first met him?

I see Jeffrey talking to another orderly, the same one who took my clothes. I don't know if I actually see it or if I imagine it, but it looks like Jeffrey keeps glancing at me while he talks. I see the other orderly smirk and possibly glance over at me too. I want to get up and confront them, but I don't. Part of me isn't around.

Why isn't he here? Is it because he is only a figment of my imagination? Because he never really existed? Or are the meds actually working for the first time in forever?

I remind myself that is why I'm at Trinity. To get rid of Abel. To get rid of my dark side. To come back to reality, bury any figments of my imagination and leave them to rot. To cleanse myself of the memories. Pieces of my past that resulted in Abel's arrival.

Eating some grits, I chuckle to myself. It's funny, I think, that I can remember the first time I met Abel, beating the shit out of some asshole who couldn't take no for an answer when it came to some girl my aunt planned to adopt back when I was a teenager. I can remember all of that, but I can't remember most of last night.

"Hey, James…"

I snap to attention just as Lance sits across from me. I nod before taking another sip of my coffee. He asks, "How are you doing?"

I give a shrug followed by another sip or two of coffee. Lance continues, "I saw you sitting over here by yourself and I thought, why not go and sit with the guy? He's new. He doesn't know anybody. No point in him being alone."

A tiny grin forms from my lips. "I appreciate it, Lance. I do. I've had a rough morning. I woke up and couldn't remember a damn thing from last night. My head was splitting, and I threw up. I fell out of my bed, going face first into my own vomit," I say, using my hands to animate what happened, slamming one on the table.

"You remember meeting me, so that's a plus," Lance says with a grin of his own.

"That's the thing," I begin, "I barely remember that. I barely remember therapy. I can see myself sitting with the group, but nothing that was said. Did I say anything? And how about you? Are you having any issues remembering?"

Lance's smile has faded as he shakes his head, "No, no. I remember plenty from last night. I don't get why you don't."

"That's what I'm trying to understand myself, Lance."

He faintly chortles, looking at me like I'm crazy, which I find funny because we are both in a mental institution. Lance replies, "Look, we had therapy. We had dinner. You and I met in the hallway where we spoke for a few moments. I told you to not let this place get to you, which apparently isn't working. After our conversation, you went into your room, and it was lights out. There is nothing complicated about it."

I roll my eyes, "Oh yeah, there's not a damn thing complicated about it, except for the fact that I can't remember most of it. I don't know about you, but I sure as shit find that more than a little strange. Wouldn't you?"

Lance looks at me then around at the other patients before squinting over at Jeffrey and the other orderly. I snap my fingers and his gaze meets mine. "Is Jeffrey a good guy?" I ask. Lance looks back at Jeffrey before looking at me once again, and he nods.

"What about the other guy?"

"Steve?"

"Yeah, Steve. Sure. Is Steve a good guy?"

Lance groans, "Maybe sitting with you was a mistake, James."

I watch as he gets up, grabbing his tray of food, before disappearing into the sea of scrubs and patients. I catch sight of him again. This time, Lance talks with Jeffrey and Steve. They all look at me for a second or two. Jeffrey and Steve nod before Lance's head and shoulders hunker down and he makes an exit. Jeffrey and Steve look over at me before looking at one another, getting lost in a conversation. I wish I could be a fly on the wall as they talk.

I wish that Abel was around, as well. That's another funny thing, I tell myself, that I came here to get rid of him, yet my second day in, and I already need the bastard. I know if Abel was around, he would be laughing his ass off, and right now, I know I'd be okay with that.

Being alone scares me.

Being alone doesn't last forever.

14

Breakfast ends and we all break off into groups, going in different directions before I find myself in a room as group therapy begins. Dr. McIntosh is seated as we enter the room. Dressed in a white button-up shirt and a tie, with gray slacks covering crossed legs, he wears a smile on his face, presenting himself to us as the epitome of comfort.

"Good morning folks. How are we on this lovely morning?" he asks. There are a few mumbles and faint groans mixed in with fake smiles and nods. I do neither as I take my seat. McIntosh plants both feet on the ground, his notebook under his right arm as he peers at us, looking at each patient one by one as if he is wearing special glasses while trying to get a read on each individual, the glasses giving something away about us. "Looks like a lot of sleepy people in here."

More mumbles and groans. More fake smiles and nods. More silence from me. McIntosh speaks again, "Alright ladies and gents. Let's all rise up," he says before climbing to his feet, lifting his arms high above his head. "Let's stretch things out a bit." I watch as everyone else gets to their feet. Not wanting to give away the fact that I am questioning things due to my memory loss, I join in. I stretch high above my head, reaching for the stars as McIntosh instructs us to do. "Alright, let's get the blood pumping!" McIntosh shouts with such vigor before his body alternates into jumping jacks. We all do the same, showing him just what good sheep we are.

In the middle of the exercise, I can't help but wonder if Abel is still in my head. I am questioning so much, just as he was when he found out my plan to check into a facility. Before I can continue my internal interrogation, McIntosh speaks again, asking us to be seated. We do as we are told. McIntosh smiles at all of us. "Alright, I hope everyone feels alive and awake now. I want us to have a big discussion today. I want everyone to open up. I don't want anyone to feel shy or afraid. Remember," he says, taking another look around the circle, "this place is your own personal Wonderland. There are no judgments." Hearing him call it a Wonderland causes my hands to form fists almost instantly. I cross my arms over my chest to hide them.

"Anyone?" McIntosh asks. "Anyone at all?"

Finally, someone raises their hands. His name is Thomas. He's a little round in the middle, with a doughy face and brown eyes. By the looks of his arms and wrists, he is a frequent visitor to suicide attempts. He tells us that he tried to kill himself a few days before coming to Trinity, stating that watching the news gave him the sense there was no real hope, so he took a razor to his arms. Thomas clarifies that it wasn't just another sort of razor. He tells us that he used a disposable razor, before pointing to the scars that will never go away running up and down his arms, around his ankles, and even his neck.

Thomas finishes his story. I listen as he and McIntosh speak. Other patients join in the discussion before Thomas tells us that he is just happy to be alive. Then, they clap. Even I join in. Once things settle, McIntosh asks if anyone else would like to speak. I finally raise my hand. McIntosh looks over at me. "Ah, yes. James, would you like to share?"

I nod, clear my throat, shift back and forth in my seat as I feel nervous suddenly, like a kid in school who raises his hand to answer a question, only to forget the answer and the question. Taking a deep breath and following it with a sigh I say, "I'm not ready to talk about why I decided to come here." I lock eyes with McIntosh, "I'd like to talk about something else, if that's alright…."

McIntosh nods. "Absolutely, James. The floor is all yours."

"So, to get to the point, I've had a rough morning," I state with a slight snicker, "and I don't know about the rest of you, but I can't seem to remember a damn thing from last night. Has anyone else had that issue today? Or maybe your first night here? But then again," I shake my head, "If you did, you wouldn't be able to remember."

I look around at the other patients. They all look at McIntosh then at one another, but no one looks at me, which puzzles me. I lean forward in my seat. "Am I the only one who is having this issue?" I ask, my question sounding more like a plea than anything else.

McIntosh speaks, causing me to make eye contact. "James, I'm sure there have been many patients who have dealt with what you're dealing with right now. You call it memory loss, just as they did. I call it something else."

I feel my teeth grind together as I reply, "And what do you call it, Doc?"

McIntosh clears his throat and adjusts his glasses. "It, like it was for them, is your way of suppressing things."

"What would I have to suppress about coming here to get help?"

He shrugs. "Plenty of things. You had to give away your belongings, so that could have triggered something. Being away from loved ones. The fact that maybe you're not quite ready to be here. That could be another factor. Your mind is trying to deal with all these new things. A new place. New faces. Everything is brand new, James, and your mind is trying to catch up to the changes you've made so unexpectedly."

I try to process his response, but I end up shaking my head. "No. I don't think that's it at all. I didn't have this issue at Vaughn. I don't understand why I'm having it here and now."

McIntosh answers, "No one can understand why things happen the way they do, James. I don't expect you to do so, just as you shouldn't expect your body to react the same way it did a few years ago. Different times create different situations; therefore, different reactions are generated. Does that make sense?"

I don't know how to react to his statement. It doesn't make sense. I want to scream but I keep it to myself. I feel like he is trying to minimize things. I tell myself that I'm not being crazy. Am I? Or is McIntosh telling me the truth? Is he being honest? Is this all in my head?

15

"James?"

I realize I am staring down at the floor, rocking back and forth in my chair ever so slightly as I look at McIntosh once again. "Are you alright?"

"I'm not really sure."

He smiles. "That is why you are here. I am here to help you, just as I am here to help everyone else in this room. In this facility. You just have to let me in."

I swallow, looking up, down, and around before my eyes meet McIntosh's, I breathe in and out, in and out, trying to quiet my thoughts before I ask, "What do you want to know?"

McIntosh clears his throat once more and looks up at the ceiling, as if he is pondering something. Like we are in a game of chess and he is plotting his next move. A few moments pass before our eyes meet again and McIntosh states, "I want you to tell me what you think or feel is the reason behind all of your anger."

Silence enters the room after he stops speaking. It is to the point that you could hear a pin drop. Being asked what I think is the reason behind my anger is a question I have heard and answered more times than I count. Each person behind the question has been as different as my response. I tell myself that I can conjure up a new lie and see where that takes me before telling myself each lie has led me to a place like this.

Do I really want to live out the rest of my days in Trinity, or a place just like it? I close my eyes as I let out a sigh. I ask myself what created the anger I have inside. So many thoughts and faces travel through my mind, starting off fast like a roller coaster but slowly dying down as it does when the ride ends. When everything comes to a stop, I only see one face. I open my eyes as I say, "My father. He is the reason behind all of my anger. Everything started because of him."

"Are you sure?" McIntosh asks. I assume he does this because he's read my file. I'm sure he's seen the inconsistencies of my stories, which have ranged from not getting what I want all the way to drinking booze and popping pills. Each therapist receives a new lie. McIntosh, despite my hesitation, is going to get the truth, because as they say, the truth shall set you free.

And, that is what I want.

I want to be free.

"Yes, I'm sure," I say firmly, hoping he hears and sees my honesty.

"Okay then," McIntosh replies, "tell me why you see it as your father, instead of not getting what you want or what you feel you are owed. Tell me why it's your father instead of drugs and alcohol."

Memories flood my mind as I look down at my feet. My hands block my view and I see that I am twiddling my thumbs. Just like my grandfather. They go around and around in circles as I let the memories take me. Memories that begin from the time I was four all the way until I was 18. Memories that I have kept buried deep, allowing the ghosts to revisit any time they want, telling me that nothing ever really stays dead. I see my father standing in a room in my head as all the memories swirl around him, taking me back to the times of pain and sadness. I see all of it, with him at the very center, and then I look up.

"My father was a drunk. He was a cold-hearted son of a bitch," I begin, memories flashing in my head, sometimes in front of me, like the dots in the upper corner of a movie when the reel needs to be switched on the projector. "He would get drunk or high and he would become so tunnel-minded…" My voice begins to break up as the memories continue to overflow. "If he wanted something, he would do all that he could to get it. If anything got in his way, there would be hell to pay."

"What sort of hell, James?" McIntosh asks.

"My mother wouldn't give him sex or go to the store for more beer most of the time. He didn't like that at all. So, he would beat her, and if I tried to intervene, I would get hit as well," I say, biting my bottom lip to avoid the tears that wanted to fall. "I remember him coming from a party that he had gone to straight from work and demanding that my mother give him money to go to the store. She refused. My mom was sitting on the couch at the time. My father became so pissed off that he flipped the couch over while my mom was pregnant with my siblings…" I pause, as the very mention of my brother and sister, Logan and Holly, causes me to recount the shit our father did to them. I catch my breath before continuing, "My mom got out of the way and climbed over the couch. My father went after her. I remember jumping on his leg." My voice breaks again. "I was seven at the time. My father looked at me before driving his steel-toed boot into my ribs, sending me flying. I ended up hitting my head on the rock going around the fireplace."

I feel frozen in time. The room turns into the living room of my childhood home. The patients disappear. I see my father climb off the couch, and his mouth moves but there is no sound. He is screaming for my mother. I remember this. McIntosh is across from me as I say, "My dad kicked me so hard and I ended up cracking the back of my head." I look down, seeing myself as a child with a pool of blood pouring out from behind my head. "I had blacked out upon impact. I woke up in the hospital."

When I finish my statement, I am back at Trinity with everyone else. McIntosh looks at me. "What do you remember from the hospital?"

"I remember waking up for a split second or two to see an X-Ray of my brain but then I blacked out again. When I woke up, I had been in the hospital for two days. My father was there. He apologized before begging me to tell the doctors that I fell. He told me if I didn't, then social services when come and take me away. I wanted to be away from him, but I couldn't be away from my mother."

"And what did you do?"

I sigh, "The doctors as well as the police came to visit me. Social services came around as well. I told them all the same story. They all received the same lie."

McIntosh takes a few notes before asking, "What was your lie?"

Another sigh escapes my lungs. "I told them that my parents were in the kitchen cooking dinner and that I had been a huge fan of Spider-man at the time. I told them I had climbed onto the couch, planning to jump from the couch onto the table. I said when I jumped, I landed on the table, but I slipped, crashing into the fireplace. I told them I didn't remember much else."

"Did they believe you?"

I swallow. "I think they didn't have much of a choice. They had to go by what I said. I told the same exact story. Didn't change a thing about it. I could tell they wanted me to tell the truth, but I wouldn't. I didn't want to be taken away. I guess you could say that was when I learned how to keep the truth hidden."

I watch as McIntosh scribbles a bit more in his notepad before he locks eyes with me once more. "Can you recall the first time you were angry and used that anger? Like when you suddenly became violent? Do you have any recollection of the first time that became an issue?"

I sigh once more. "I'm not sure I want to talk about that." I shake my head as the words make their exit, shaking it as if it will get rid of the memory slowly creeping into my mind.

"You can't make any progress if you don't confront the demons of your past, James. You've been doing well today. Don't stop now," McIntosh says. I take a few deep breaths, finally letting the memory consume me as I close my eyes for a few moments. When I reopen them, as it was with the memory where my father kicked me, I am no longer in the white room with all the other patients. I am back in my middle school. I can tell by the dull gray of the hallways, from the walls to the rotating triangle pattern going across the floor.

I can see the rusty red of the lockers as I make my way through the hall, bumping shoulders with every student in the school. The further I travel, the more I realize what memory this is. I realize what is about to happen, but I can't do anything to stop it when it does. Before I know it, I am being shoved into the bathroom door. I remember I am about to experience what so many kids who walk through the doors of Liberty Rock Middle School did.

Falling through the door, I land on the wet, dull blue floor. I quickly scramble to my feet as I find myself staring into the eyes of my attacker, Dewayne Brandis. Dewayne is tall and muscular, way more than I am at this point in my life. Dewayne is two years older than me but has been held back, so we're in the same grade.

Dewayne walks in, followed by his two best friends, Jack and Leo. They are my age and about the same size as me. They're also as afraid of Dewayne as I am. Reliving the memory, I can still feel the fear I did when all of this took place.

"Look who it is…" Dewayne snickers.

"What do you want, Dewayne?" I ask, trying to keep eye contact with Dewayne. My dad always told me to look someone in the eye no matter the situation.

He shrugs. "Nothing, really. I just saw you and was immediately annoyed by your fucking presence, James. I decided I needed to do something about it."

"I haven't done anything to you," I say, trying to swallow that fear.

Dewayne shakes his head. "Are you sure about that? Because," he cackles a bit as he looks at Jack and Leo before facing me once again, "I feel like you have done something to me."

Still trying hard to get rid of my fear, I swallow before asking, "What did I do to you?"

Dewayne steps closer, placing his hand on my shoulder as he stares deep into my eyes. "You were born, you little faggot."

Before I can reply, a voice in my head speaks. "He's going to punch you." I have no time to react as Dewayne drives his fist into my stomach and the breath leaves my body. I crumple to the floor, clutching my abdomen, trying to catch my breath as I hear the voice once again, "Get up. Fight back. Get up. Fight back."

"Oh my God!" Dewayne exclaims. "You're such a little bitch. That was one hit and you're already on the ground. You make this too easy."

The voice repeats, "Get up. Fight back. Get up. Fight back."

But I do nothing. Dewayne begins to kick me over and over. Before I know it, Jack and Leo join in on the fun. The voice continues to tell me to get up and fight back. I begin to move, but not to fight back. I military crawl away, taking a beating along the way, before finally getting into one of the stalls. I manage to lock the door.

They bang and shake the door as I crawl onto the toilet, drawing my knees to my chest.

Dewayne speaks. "You're such a pussy. Just like your mommy always wanted you to be. Too bad you're not tough like your old man. If you were like your dad, maybe I wouldn't beat on you...I wouldn't beat on you like he does."

I feel tears forming in my eyes when I hear the voice speak again. The voice sounds like mine if I'd smoked heavily for fifty years. "Don't cry. You need to get up and fight. That piece of shit needs his mouth shut."

I whisper, "I don't know if I can do it. He's bigger than me."

"You don't have to," the voice replies. "I can take care of it for you."

"Are you in there, faggot?" Dewayne bangs on the door some more, with Jack and Leo beating on the stall walls. "Come on, James. Come out of there.

Fight me like your dad would. Don't be such a bitch. Leave that to your mom. I know your dad beats on her because she's too chicken shit to defend herself."

The voice shouts this time. "Get up! Fight back!"

My heart pounds and my hands form fists as I climb off the toilet. I rear back with my left leg before kicking the stall door open as everything turns black. I catch flashes here and there. I see the faces of Jack and Leo, covered in blood. Tears streaming down their faces.

I see Dewayne clutching his arm and I notice bone. Tears running red on his face as he kicks his legs to get away from me. I see flashes of my hands. The skin around the knuckles is peeled back, blood covering my hands as they reach out toward Dewayne before teachers rush in, grabbing me.

16

When they grab me, I find myself back in the white, orderlies from Trinity rushing towards me. Grabbing at me. I see my fists flying and connecting with their faces. Flashes enter my line of sight. Not of memories, but of Abel's face. He is smirking. With each flash, his smirk widens, forming into a grin.

I see the other patients backing away, cowering. I see McIntosh screaming at me. I hear nothing, but I can read his lips as they say, "James. Stop."

More hands grab me. Arms locking with mine as others grab my waist and legs, driving me to the floor. I see McIntosh out of the corner of my eye. He stomps toward me, pulling out a syringe, driving the needle into a vial of crimson liquid. He steps closer, and Abel's face stops flashing before me. McIntosh drops to one knee beside me, and the needle pierces my skin. It doesn't take long after McIntosh gets to his feet for the room to begin spinning.

It looks like I am falling from all of those around me, reminding me of the dream with Braelynn and Sophie. Like that dream, I fall until darkness fills my eyes.

When I wake, my head feels like it is being split — like wood meeting the blade of an axe. The pain feels all too familiar, along with the feeling of sickness bouncing around in my stomach. My eyes feel like they will pop out of my skull if I so much as blink or look around.

I lie in my bed, paralyzed for a few moments. I manage to look around, ignoring the ache in my pupils, and see that I am in my room. Memories begin to flood my mind, causing the splitting in my head to switch into hyper-drive. I remember my morning, feeling what I am feeling now. I remember having the awkward breakfast with Lance, just as I remember going to therapy, just as I remember talking about my father, but then everything goes blank.

I don't recall anything that happened from my confession. I also don't remember coming back to my room, so how did I get back here? The more I think or try to remember, the sicker I feel. I strain my eyes, the pain increasing as I try to force a memory, but my brain produces nothing. In between moments of fighting down the sickness trying to slither up my throat, I ask myself why I've been having such a hard time with remembering.

Is McIntosh right? Is it my way of suppressing things? What would I have to suppress from therapy? Besides, McIntosh should be helping me avoid the suppression of anything. I remind myself that he's told me I need to be open. I chuckle, once again ignoring the ache coursing through my skull as I tell myself how funny it is that I can remember things like that, but not how I ended up in my room.

I even recall hearing tales of patients becoming so overwhelmed with emotions that they black out or get incredibly sick to their stomachs. Is that what happened to me? If so, why the hell can't I remember a damned thing?

Suddenly, I hear the twist of a lock, metal grinding against metal. My thoughts cease, but the pain doesn't. The door to my room opens and McIntosh steps in, followed by orderlies I don't remember ever seeing.

He looks at me and asks, "Are you alright, James?"

I hear concern in his voice, but I feel if I open my mouth I'm going to puke again, so I give a slight nod. He looks to the orderlies and nods at them before they step out of the room, closing the door behind them.

McIntosh stares down at me as he says, "James…" he shakes his head, "you don't look so good, son."

I manage to mutter, "I don't feel so good, either."

McIntosh sighs as he crosses his arms over his chest, taking a step closer, peering at me as his glasses drop slightly off the bridge of his nose. "Do you remember anything that happened?"

A cough escapes my lungs as I say, "I don't remember a damned thing up to a certain point. That is twice in the last two days that I can't remember a certain period."

"What's the last thing you remember?"

I manage to sit up in my bed, feeling nauseous, but I'm maintaining. "I remember being in therapy. I remember you being able to get me to talk about my father. And from there, it's all a blur. How the hell does that happen, honestly?"

He shrugs. "I told you, James. It is your mind's way of suppressing things."

"That's what I don't understand. What's there for me to suppress? I was just sharing with the group. I was opening up, trying to make the best of my time here, and yet all I get for it…is what? Fucking amnesia? How do you explain that one?"

"Your mind is still trying to cope. I'd say that you're adjusting to where you are, just as your mind is trying to adjust to you opening up," McIntosh states. "You've never been willing to open up before, according to your file. When you were at the Vaughn Institute, it took you weeks to finally get motivated. You've been here two days, and you opened up. I'd call that progress, at least."

"I don't know why you're so damned cheery about it, Doc. I can't remember any of it. That doesn't sound like progress. More like regression, if you ask me," I fire back.

He sighs again, pushing his glasses up onto his nose. "Well, it's funny that you say that word." He locks eyes with me. "Regression."

"What do you mean?"

"I said that you opened up and then, from what you're describing, you lost time or blacked out. You can't remember anything. You did regress, James."

"Did something happen?" I ask, afraid to know the answer.

McIntosh nods. "Yes, James. Something did happen. You attacked people. Are you sure you don't remember any of that?"

I shake my head, ignoring the pain shooting from my neck down through my neck and spine. "What happened?"

"I don't want to trigger you, James," McIntosh says.

"I'm already triggered. I'm upset, Doc." I reply, still shaking my head, telling myself that I am never going to get better. I take a few deep breaths before meeting McIntosh's gaze. "Just tell me what happened. Please."

"Alright. I asked you to describe your earliest memory of becoming violent. You spoke of being attacked in a bathroom while you were in middle school. You spoke of how one of the bullies insulted you and your family before he punched you. You described his friends joining in as they beat you before you managed to crawl away. You talked about hearing a voice, telling you to get up and fight back. You talked about blacking out or losing time, only catching glimpses of their crying faces covered in blood, just as your hands were covered in blood before some teachers charged into the bathroom and grabbed you."

McIntosh stops, removing his glasses as he looks down and away from me. He lets out another sigh before placing his glasses back on as he turns to me. "And then, before I knew it, you became enraged. You started attacked patients. When the orderlies tried to restrain you, you attacked them. You became an entirely different person."

I know who he is talking about as soon as he says it.

He continues, "Once they were able to restrain you, I had to give you a sedative. That is how you got back here." He looks at me, and I can see a hint of frustration in his eyes, but I say nothing. "Do you not remember any of that?" I shake my head. He sighs before slowly backing towards the door. "James, I know you have issues and I am here to work with you, but I cannot allow that to happen again. If you become violent once more, I will have you placed in solitary."

I say nothing, not having the slightest clue as to what I can say in response to what he told me. I bury my face in my hands after he leaves the room, trying to comprehend that I attacked people. Innocent people.

I curse myself, pressing my fingernails into my skin ever so gently, fighting the urge to dig them in deeper, to tear at my flesh, when I hear Abel's voice.

"You didn't attack anyone."

I slowly bring my hands from my face. I look up to see Abel standing near the spot where McIntosh stood. He looks just as frustrated as McIntosh did.

"I know that I didn't attack anyone," I say, "You did. You're the one with the thirst for violence."

Abel shakes his head. "I am you and you are me. I have told you this before. My thirst for violence is actually yours, James. You've kept it bottled up, and I am what happens when the pressure builds to the point where the lid pops off."

"I had no reason to attack anyone here, Abel."

He sighs. "I just told you that you didn't attack anyone, James. McIntosh is filling your head full of lies. He wants you to believe his every word. He wants you to think you're crazy."

"And maybe I am," I say, wanting to bite and swallow my tongue for thinking that.

Abel grows silent for a few moments. I watch as he paces back and forth, however, before he speaks once again. "I told you that coming here was a bad idea. It was a huge mistake. We could have worked things out on our own, James. We didn't need to come to a place like this."

"I tried for weeks to work this out on my own," I roar, "and what ended up happening? I hurt someone. Just like you wanted."

The memory comes back. I see myself attacking someone I considered a friend and a colleague. I see myself bashing his nose into the floor. Seeing it reminds me of how much control I've never really had.

"I did it because you wanted to, James. Don't make me out to be the monster because you're too much of a chickenshit to take responsibility for your own actions," Abel states, grinding his teeth.

"You are a monster, Abel! I know what you've had me do!" I bellow before slowly rising to my feet. "You've had me do things that nearly cost me my family. Things that should have landed me in prison!"

Abel rolls his eyes. "I don't know if you've noticed, but this place is prison! They shaved your head. They took away your belongings and made you dress in scrubs. That screams 'prison' to me. I don't know about you, but then again, you like to be clueless as to what is going on."

"What the hell are you talking about?"

Abel runs his hands over his scarred face, exhaling deeply as he replies, "I told you that you didn't attack anyone. McIntosh told you differently. He said you attacked other patients and orderlies. I am in your head, James. I know what goes on, yet you believe that walking crock of shit."

"Because he's trying to help me. You've caused me nothing but pain, Abel."

Pain shoots through my body, causing me to collapse back onto the bed. I groan as I clutch my abdomen and my head as it begins to split in different directions once again. I squeeze my temples with all that I have, hoping the pain succumbs to the pressure and breaks away.

I hear Abel as he says, "I know what I have done... what we have done... in the past, James. You're a better person than you were all those years ago. I've told you this makes me a better person. I only came back because I want to protect you. The pain you're feeling now is from McIntosh. He did give you medicine, but it's not what he said it was. I wish you would believe me. For once."

Still squeezing, I pray for the pain to end, for Abel to go away, for it all just to go away. "I don't know what to believe anymore."

I close my eyes, trying to think of something good. I dig into my mind, going as deep as I possibly can, searching for happiness. I see my daughter's smile. I hear her laugh, but these things seem to only be temporary as they fade quicker than they arrive. I see my wife. I see us walking through the city, hand in hand, laughing and joking around. I see us going out to dinner. I see us enjoying our meals before the restaurant is engulfed in flames, burning anything and everything, burning the memory away.

I see myself reaching for Braelynn's hand as she turns to me, concern and sadness in her eyes. I reach for her hand, but there is nothing for me to touch. She becomes flame, then ash. I do the same just as I open my eyes. I am still in my room. Abel is gone, but I am still here. I shake my head, telling myself I don't want to be here.

I repeat it over and over again.

I don't want to be here. I don't want to be here. I don't want to be here.

17

I close my eyes, waiting for a memory to surface. I just want to be anywhere but here right now. I see myself in the bathroom, in middle school. My hands covered in blood. Teachers rushing in and grabbing me. I see myself in the lobby next to the principal's office. My mother arrives, leaving me to sit in the lobby alone. I see her come out of the office, tears in her eyes as she tells me to come with her. I see myself, my eyes filled with hesitation before I slowly follow her, the hesitation growing into fear.

I see myself sitting on a couch in an office. I see a man sitting before me, but not his face. I can tell it's a man by the hands that grip his notebook and pen. When he speaks, his voice is muffled yet it echoes, a boom behind each word.

I see a golden pocket watch with the outline of a spider on the back of it, swinging back and forth. I see my eyes darting in rhythm with it before I lie down on the couch. The man gets up. He disappears out of view for a few moments. When he returns, he has a syringe filled with a pale green liquid as he towers over me, bringing the needle closer and closer.

My eyes shoot open as I sit up in bed, gasping for breath. This time, I can no longer fight it. The sickness emerges.

The door to my room opens and I wake up in alarm. The last memory I have is of the man without a face standing above me when I was a child, driving a syringe toward me. The length of the needle is fresh in my mind, causing me to bolt from my bed, standing guard for whoever is on the other side of the door.

I see McIntosh enter with a few orderlies in tow. I lower my guard, but only slightly. McIntosh and the orderlies form a triangle around me. I lock eyes with each of them before speaking to McIntosh. "Is something wrong?"

The good doctor sighs. "James, I've come to share some news with you." He clears his throat as I do my best to not fear the worst, and then he says, "I've come to tell you that I am going to move you from this building into another one."

"Which building is that?"

He clears his throat again. "Building X6, or the building in the back as I pointed out on your first day. Do you remember this conversation?"

Of the few things I have remembered since coming here, this is one of them. I nod. "Yes, I remember. But...why am I being moved? I've done nothing wrong, plus those patients have killed people. I've done nothing of the sort, Doc."

McIntosh nods his head. "Yes, I know that. You've never taken the life of another, but you are a danger to yourself and others, especially in this building. You are what I call a level 6, hence the name of the building. X6."

"How am I a danger? You said I attacked patients and orderlies yesterday. That was only once. You even said that if it happened again, I would have to be moved. So far, it hasn't happened again. I think what you're doing is wrong. I think you're wrong, therefore I shouldn't have to move." I press my back against the wall, keeping my eyes on everyone else in the room, not knowing what to expect, but wanting to be prepared.

"James," McIntosh exhales, "I know what I said. I was here when I said it. When I left yesterday, I maintained my hopes things would progress for you, but then I heard you talking. I came back and stood outside of your door. I watched you. I heard you. You were having conversations with yourself, or this voice in your head. And do you know what that showed me?"

I shrug. "No. What did it show you, Doc?"

"It showed me that you are suffering from a mental break. With someone with violent tendencies, such as yourself, I know you are a risk. I know that your behavior is unpredictable. Therefore, I don't know if you can be trusted around my staff or the other patients."

I shake my head. "If that is the case, then I would very much like to leave your facility, Doc. I can leave whenever I choose, remember?"

McIntosh grins, and I get a bad feeling immediately. "Actually, James," I feel my heart sick into the pit of sickness resonating in my stomach, "you signed paperwork which indicated that we are legally allowed to keep you up to seven days. After that point, if we feel like you are able to return to society, then you may go. But, if we feel you're not, we have legal authority to retain you until the time comes that you're able to re-enter the outside world."

"He's fucking with you, James," Abel says, his voice creeping up my spine. "Don't give into it. He wants you to let me loose. I'd love nothing more than to rip his throat out, but now isn't the time."

"Why wouldn't I be able to return to my life outside of these walls?" I ask, trying to remain calm, trying to listen to Abel's good advice.

A heavy sigh escapes McIntosh's lips. "James, I just explained this to you. You're a danger to yourself and others. You've made progress, yes, but you take one step forward then four or five steps back. Talking to yourself or this violent personality of yours, and then," he pauses, lifting a finger as he glares at me, "you attack innocent people because you cannot control your rage. That alone shows just how unfit for society you are, James."

"He wants you to attack him, James...." Abel says. "Don't do it. I can feel that you want to, because I want to, but I can't."

Abel's actually trying to be the voice of reason for once.

He is right. I want to hurt McIntosh. Holding me here against my will. He's fed me lie after lie. Every time I lied to a therapist is coming back to haunt me, I think to myself.

"I want to see the papers I signed," I say, the feeling of losing control rushing through my body. I take a deep breath to hold it back. "I want to see them!" I shout, placing my hands behind my back so they cannot be seen forming fists.

McIntosh stares at me for a few moments, taking me back to that feeling of being in a chess match. "Fine, James. You can see them."

In his hand is a blue plastic binder, which he opens before pulling out a file. He placed the file on top of the binder, flips through it, and pulls out a couple of papers. He hands them to one of the orderlies, who passes it off to me.

My eyes scan them as McIntosh speaks. "You see, James? I'm not lying to you despite what thoughts your broken mind may or may not be producing in that head of yours."

I say nothing. I want to tear the papers to shreds, but I don't. I hand them back, losing faith in this place, wanting to escape from this Wonderland. Reading those forms, I tell myself that I've gone down the rabbit hole with no way out. I look at McIntosh, the good doctor, and there are so many things I want to say, that I want to do, but nothing comes out.

Abel tells me "Be patient, James."

McIntosh clears his throat, looks at his watch, and then he looks at me. "Alright, James. I will have some orderlies come to get you in order to transport you across campus to your new room in the next half hour. I do not want any issues out of this. Is that understood?"

I say nothing. I just return to my bed and sit. He looks at me some more before shaking his head and making his exit.

I sit in my room, just waiting.

Waiting for McIntosh to return with more bad news. Something else that he can say or do to fuck with me. I ask myself if he is only testing me. I know it is a possibility, but so far, it seems like there is nothing for sure when it comes to McIntosh...or the ship he runs at Trinity.

I think back to my first day, how McIntosh hesitated when I mentioned leaving whenever I wanted. The way he played it off irked me then. Today, I learned the ugly truth behind his hesitation, and I am beyond irked.

I tell myself that I should have let Abel seize control. That he should have ruined McIntosh, even if the orderlies would have gotten involved.

"What good would that have done, James?" Abel asks.

I reply, talking as low as I can, not looking towards Abel as he sits in the far corner of the room, not wanting to appear any crazier than McIntosh has already made me out to be. "I don't know, Abel. I really don't. I can't help but find it utterly hilarious how you are the voice of reason suddenly. You used to want me to hurt people. Now, when I want to..." I pause, repeating the words 'When I want to' in my head a few times before I continue, "you suddenly become scared."

Abel shakes his head, sighing in the process. "You know that I am not scared of anything, especially when it comes to hurting people. But where we are, James...this isn't the place to let that out. They have us on lockdown already. Your life... OUR lives... are resting in the palm of McIntosh's hand. He controls everything. He's the puppet master."

I sigh as well. "So, what? Do I just play by his rules? Do what Lance said? Not let this place get me down?"

"Sounds like great advice to me," Abel states.

Before I can reply, my door opens. I look up to see Jeffrey standing there with Steve behind him. Jeffrey waves at me. "Hey, James. How are you, man?"

"I've been better," I say, standing to my feet. "I take it that you're moving me."

Jeffrey nods. "Yes sir, I am. But hey, don't let it get you down. You'll be out of there in no time. Dr. McIntosh has high hopes for you, James. I know it may not seem like it, but he does."

Raising an eyebrow, I say, "I'm being moved into a building filled with murderers. How is that supposed to not bring me down? He may have high hopes for me, but my hopes for this place and his therapy are quickly diminishing."

Jeffrey smiles and shakes his head. "No, James. There's no need for negativity. You know how they say God has a plan for all of us?" I nod my head, trying to hide the fact I'm questioning him comparing McIntosh to God. "Dr. McIntosh has a plan for all of his patients, including you. He'll work with you and motivate you to become your best self. You just have to be open. Now if you will please follow me. Steve will walk behind you as a safety precaution," Jeffrey says as he switches from his jolly self to all business.

18

I do as I am told, following Jeffery as we exit my room, entering a long corridor before walking through what appears to me as a glass tunnel, connecting the current building to another across the campus. Upon entry and exit of the tunnel, Jeffrey uses his badge, which he says is for security purposes before giving me a wink.

"Welcome to Facility X6," Jeffrey says. I can tell by the tone of his voice that he is trying to make it seem like something it's not. Like I should be happy to be here. I say nothing. I only follow him, with Steve still in tow.

As we enter the building, I am immediately overtaken by the smell. This isn't Wonderland. This is a slum. This is an alleyway constantly flooded by an ever-falling rain, washing the filth of the surrounding city, with the water and dirt soaking into the concrete, the brick of the buildings, into everything. It smells rotten to its very core, and as far as I can tell, I am in the rotten core of all things Trinity.

X6 is filled with rust. It covers the six levels of the building. Rust on the railing, the stairwells, and the grates beneath our feet as we continue our journey. It is on the walls, and in the holding cells, where I soon find myself. There is no door. Only bars, like I am in a fucking prison. I stand near the doorway of my cell as Steve pushes the bars closed. I lock eyes with Jeffrey. "So, what is this shit? What happened to Trinity being our own personal Wonderland?"

"When you're not opening yourself to the experience, then nothing is a Wonderland. It all becomes a prison."

"This is prison. Just look at it," I say.

Jeffrey nods, "This building was used as an offset prison. I mean, prisons are becoming overcrowded as it is. Crime runs rampant, producing more prisoners than there are prisons, so places like this have been used. Prisoners aren't meant to live a life of luxury. They lost that right when they decided to commit crimes such as murder, James."

I look around, feeling my jaw tighten up. I see several of the prisoners in their cells, some of them looking away, others looking straight at me. I turn to Jeffrey. "I want out of here."

Jeffrey nods once more. "I know, man. And I don't like bringing anyone here, but I have to follow orders. It could help you to do the same, James. From what I've seen and heard, you like to question everything. You like to go against McIntosh's recommendations. You hurt people. You're fighting the experience."

I go to say something but all that comes is a punch against the bars before I turn away. I look down at my hand. The knuckles are already swelling as a bruise begins to surface. I don't know how long I look at my hand but by the time I turn around again, Jeffrey and Steve are gone. I look around before sitting on my bed.

"Hey man..." A voice says, coming from over my shoulder. I turn to see a ghostly white man staring back at me. His hair is stringy and red, like he hasn't bathed in only God knows how long. "Oh, I didn't mean to frighten you."

"You didn't scare me," I state, cutting him off as I look straight ahead, doing my best to avoid eye contact.

"Well, this place can scare anyone. I've been scared a time or two myself, and I've murdered at least six people. Couple of animals, too. I did it all for shits and giggles." I grind my teeth as he continues, "It started with my best friend before I moved onto his wife and kids." He coughs and all I can think about are Braelynn and Sophie. My wife. My daughter. He speaks again, "He had everything that I ever wanted, so I decided to take it all away."

I bolt from the bed, almost dragging it with me. I turn to him, glaring. "Just shut the fuck up. I don't want to hear a damned thing that you have to say, you insane piece of shit."

He laughs, slapping his leg in the process. He is seated on his bed as well, rocking back and forth as he laughs. Once that dies down, we lock eyes. "We are all insane in some way. That is why we are all in here. Even you," he states, pointing at me as a grin forms on his face.

"I'm not like you," I fire back.

"Not yet," he screeches, before lying down on his bed, as an eerie silence fills this place.

I pull my bed into the center of the cell, making sure it isn't close enough to any of the cell walls. I don't want to wake up with someone like the psychopath next door reaching for my throat. Once I feel I'm safe, I rest my head onto the mattress. There is no level of comfort in X6, nor this bed. I stare out at nothing, bringing my body into the fetal position. I manage to tune out the world around me, letting it become fumes, like I have turned most everything in my life into.

This doesn't go on for long as the fumes become real life things once again and I hear a tapping followed by echoes against the bars of my cell. I look over my shoulder to find Jeffrey has returned. His ever-present smile lingers. "Hello, James. May we speak for a moment?"

"What is this about?" I ask, rising to my feet.

"Dr. McIntosh knows of our conversation. I had to tell him. There was no way around it, especially if I'd like to keep my job, which I do," he says, with a small desperate chuckle. "But he remains strong in his decision to move you here.

"Isn't he grand?"

"Very much so," Jeffrey states with an annoying enthusiasm. "He has offered a solution, however." I stare at Jeffrey curiously as he fumbles through the breast pocket of his shirt before his fingers emerge with a pill. It is red and circular, like the size of an Advil.

"What the hell is that?"

"It's medication, James. You've taken it before."

I shake my head. "No, I haven't. What are you talking about?"

"You've taken it before, James. I can promise you that. I even gave it to you," Jeffrey insists.

"I don't know what the hell you're talking about. When did you give it to me?"

"I gave it to you on your first night. Right before you went to sleep. Do you not remember?"

19

My first night? I lower my gaze as I try to force the memories. My mind travels back to my first day. I see it all, but after the conversation with Lance, nothing appears. It's all blank. Staring back at Jeffrey, who stands calm and firm, I say, "I don't remember a damn thing. You didn't give that to me."

Then, it hits me. What if he did give it to me and it was the reason behind my memory loss? Behind the vomiting?

"Is that why I can't remember anything, Jeffrey? Because of that stupid fucking pill? Tell me!" I shout, clinging to the bars, baring my teeth at him. "Tell me!"

"There are side effects of this medication, just like all other medications, James," Jeffrey says. His cool demeanor makes me want to hurt him even more. "Two of those side effects are memory loss as well as nausea. You experienced both."

I grip the bars as tight as I can, pulling them, imagining my hands tearing them apart and grabbing Jeffrey. "And you want me to take it again?"

"You don't have to. It's ultimately your choice, James. You went through the typical side effects when someone first takes it. After that, taking it is easy. Nothing really happens. It just makes you feel…" he tilts his head from side to side, "more like who you really are."

"That doesn't make me feel any better, Jeffrey. Puking my guts out and not remembering shit isn't who I am or who I want to be."

He nods. "Ah, I see." He shrugs before his eyes grow wide with a slight excitement. "What if I told you that this could help get you out of here?"

Everything changes. My grip loosens. I slowly step back, putting my fangs away. I look at the pill then at Jeffrey. "How do I know it's legit?"

"I've not told you anything but the truth since you've arrived, James. I have no reason to start doing otherwise. This pill," his eyes glance down at it before meeting mine once again, "could be your one-way ticket out of this building, and heck," childlike delight falls over his face, "it could be your ticket back home, as well. All you have to do is show a little faith."

"A little faith in what?" I ask, still hesitant.

"Faith in the process. Faith in myself. Faith in Dr. McIntosh. We all want what is best for you, James," he smiles before glancing down at the pill once again. I see it resting in the palm of his hand as he asks, "So, what is it going to be?"

I remain cautious as I step closer before another thought crosses my mind. Taking my eyes away from the pill, my so-called ticket out of here, I say, "I want my journal." Jeffrey looks at me, puzzled, but I repeat it: "I want my journal. I need my journal." He says nothing so I plead, "May I have my journal?"

Jeffrey shrugs, "I'm not sure, James. Those sorts of requests have to go through Dr. McIntosh. I can't make that decision on my own. I am sure if you take this then it will help your chances. May I ask why you want or need your journal?"

I point to my head, "It helps me keep things focused up here. I think it'd be very helpful for me."

Jeffrey nods. "Alright. Give me a reason to bring it up to Dr. McIntosh and I will definitely see what I can do." He looks at the pill then at me. I exhale deeply before reaching for the pill. I place it on the tip of my tongue, trying my damnedest to not think about the worst that can happen as I swallow it whole.

Once Jeffrey leaves, I sit on my bed and wait. I let the medicine flow through me, consuming me inside and out. Time passes me by, and I don't know how much I lose, but when I find myself looking up, I see Dr. McIntosh sitting across from me. I am not in my cell, but a closed off room. It looks like one of those interrogation rooms you see on all of those police procedural shows that litter one's television.

"What is this?" I ask, looking around.

He smiles. "Group therapy, James."

"There are no other patients, so I wouldn't call this a group necessarily," I say.

"On the contrary," McIntosh says before snapping his fingers. A light comes on to my right. There is a glass window. The light reveals new faces I've never seen before. Men and women. All of them wear white lab coats. They all have clipboards, notepads, and pens. All their eyes are on me. "We are not alone, my friend. I've brought my colleagues along."

I take another look at them, his colleagues, before looking at McIntosh. "And what is your reasoning behind that?"

He rocks back and forth in his seat before resting his elbows on the metal table positioned in between us. "You are a fascinating case, James. I'll admit that I've struggled in terms of getting a read on you. I know that you're violent and unpredictable. So far, the only conclusions I've come up with…" He pauses for a moment, adjusting his glasses, which is something I sense he does when he's nervous, and then he continues, "is that nothing is for sure when it comes to you. I don't like not being able to get a read on my patients, because it delays my ability to help them help themselves. Do you understand?"

"You gave me a pill that caused me to lose my memory. That caused me to puke all over myself and everywhere else. I can see why it's hard for you to get a read on not only me, but the rest of your patients when you're doing nothing but making them sick."

McIntosh scoffs, "If that is truly how you feel, James then I have failed you already. You have failed yourself as well. I would never do anything to any of my patients, especially something that could harm them in any way, James."

A laugh escapes me. "You're kidding me, right? You had that pill given to me. You have placed me in a cell, surrounded by people you've claimed to be murderers, among other things. I don't know about you or your fucking colleagues, but it feels like you're putting me in harm's way."

"You did take the pill Jeffrey offered you, correct?"

"Yes," I say, coldly. "He said it would help get me the hell out of X6."

"Well, it could," McIntosh replies. "You see, I've not had to move many patients to X6. I've moved them out and into another building, with a lower level of care, or even back into society."

I bypass everything he said except one thing. "You said it could. Not that it would. I don't belong in X6. I am not insane, damn it!"

"James, please. Remain calm."

I shake my head. "How in the hell do you expect me to stay calm? I've been here three damned days and it has been nothing short of a nightmare! You are unbelievable, man. You really are. With all that has happened…" I begin listing things, using my fingers, "I mean, I explain to the group how I couldn't remember a lot of my first night. I woke up puking, which I can't remember how many times I've said that, but it sure as shit is worth repeating. What's funny about that is the fact Jeffrey told me that he gave me some medication, which would have caused me to forget. Which would have caused me to get sick. You knew that all along, yet you didn't care to mention it when I brought it up in the first place."

"I wanted to see what you would do," McIntosh replies. "Jeffrey, I'm sure, told you those pills were to help you become who you really are. And so far, all I have seen is aggression, James. Being aggressive is part of who you are. Violence is in your nature. Ridding you of that aggression, of that violence, is a riddle I have struggled to solve, and I have usually gotten a read on a patient by their second day here. We are fast approaching the end of your third, and I am at a loss."

I chuckle, "Maybe you're a fucking quack, Doc. Did you ever think of that?"

McIntosh shakes his head. "Actually, no. I've not thought of that, James. I know that I am a damn good doctor. You, my friend, are a challenge, and I welcome all challenges. I will not stop until I have helped you, James."

"And how do you plan to do that? By torturing me?"

"No, sir. I do not believe in such a thing. You're in X6, remember, because you are a danger to yourself and others. So, let's talk about why you're a danger. Yesterday, before your attack against my staff and the patients, you were referring to your father as the reason behind all your anger. Do you remember this?"

"I remember talking about my father. Definitely not attacking staff or patients."

"Do you want to stay in the past, James? Or would you like to move forward? You can deny what happened all you wish, but I have proof. I have witnesses. Now, we can remain stuck on what you believe did or did not happen, or we can proceed with our session today and hope to gain some traction in terms of helping you," McIntosh states before leaning back in his seat.

"I wouldn't have come here if I didn't want to better myself and change," I hiss, "but so far nothing you've done has really given me any sort of faith in your methods. When we had therapy in your office, all you did was load me down with pills. Those helped me. Somewhat. But, here...at Trinity...it's been mind games."

"I'm not playing mind games with you, but I do want to help you with your broken mind. I want to help piece together the puzzle of your mind, and why you became the violent and aggressive person you are today. So, the next statement from you needs to either be yes or no. If you say no, then you will return to X6 and remain there until you are somehow rehabilitated. If you say yes, then we will explore all avenues into curing you," McIntosh says, crossing his legs, gripping his knee with both hands.

I stare at McIntosh for a good long while, glancing at his cohorts every so often before sighing and throwing my hands up. "What real choice do I have? I want to go home. I want some semblance of normalcy. Calling you out on your shit isn't getting me any closer to what I want. So, my answer is yes. I'm ready to begin."

"Good," McIntosh says, clicking his pen, touching the tip to the open page of his ever-present notebook. "So, as I was saying regarding your father. You've claimed him to be the reason behind your anger. Correct?"

I nod, and he continues, "Now, tell me James. Can you describe your earliest memory of your father's anger? It doesn't have to be against you, but a time where he showed anger and aggression that affected you to your very core."

He didn't even have to ask. I already know, I tell myself, as the memory digs itself up and reveals its contents to me. "I remember it like it was yesterday. I was six at the time. My mother was working a double shift at the hospital, so I was with my father all day long."

As I narrate, I can see my father sitting at the kitchen table, a few feet from me. I am eating cereal. He is drinking beer and popping pills. He looks at up at me. "You need to finish that shit. We have to get a move on. I've got places to be and people to see."

I lift a spoonful of Frosted Flakes out of the bowl, white and cracked like the walls of the kitchen due to the many wars my father waged against my mother, as well as himself. "Where do we have to go?" I ask before stuffing my face with the cereal.

"Let me worry about that," he says, taking another swig of beer before crumpling the can into a dime and tossing it near the trash can, among other empty cans and cigarette packs. I see a few cockroaches scatter. I don't let my father see how the sight of them disgusts me, because I know he would slap me for thinking that I'm better than where I live. He gets up from the table, "Alright, get up. We need to get going. I'll be in the car."

I see us driving down the highway in my father's ragtag Buick. The rust on it reminds me of everything inside of X6. The city passes us by as morning turns to mid-afternoon. The sunlight becomes cloudy, which produces rain, soaking our quiet journey through the slums and alleyways only few dared to enter. My father goes in, empty handed except for the revolver he keeps tucked in the back of his pants, but when he returns, my father, with his hardened face and sunken eyes, long, curly black hair, always has a bag of something in his hands.

"One time," I tell Dr. McIntosh, as a sorrow-filled cackle makes its way into our conversation, "I looked in the bag. I saw money and a few bricks of coke. I got a backhand for sticking my nose into business that didn't pertain to me."

I continue recounting, as everything unravels like a movie. The sun dies down as my father and I are swallowed by the darkness of night. The rusted Buick makes a stop. For the first time, my father removes his gun, checks it for bullets before popping the cylinder back in place. I watch as he gets out of the car and disappears into the dark. I stare at the bags my father has placed in the backseat floorboard. I'm tempted to check the contents, when I hear a gunshot.

I turn and look ahead, my heart pounds against my chest, my breathing becomes difficult as my lungs tighten with fear. I watch as my father emerges from the shadows, not carrying a bag, but another man. My father's fingers have twisted the collar of the man's shirt into a ball, dragging him out into the street.

"He was a black guy," I tell McIntosh, my voice shaking like my hands.

The movie continues to play as I describe it. I see my father begin pistol whipping the man, cursing him, though I'm not sure why. He hurls not only the butt of the gun at the man, but racist expletives. My father loosens his grip before kicking the man to the ground. I watch as he drives his boot into the man's ribs then his head, before my father returns the gun to the back of his pants as he heads toward the car.

I feel frozen as I stare at the lifeless body on the ground, hoping to see him move. I feel tears trying to build up in my eyes, but I fight them because I know how much my father hates to see me cry. He's called me a faggot more times than I can count.

He gets in the car, slamming the door before starting the car. "Sit the fuck down!" He says, shoving me into the seat. We peel off, leaving the body. I turn and watch, hoping for movement to occur, but it doesn't. I watch until the body becomes a speck, before it becomes nothing, fading into the night.

Silence resides in the car, as I try to process what I've just seen. I take a deep breath before looking at my father. Blood covers the hands gripping the steering wheel. I trace from his hands, over his arms, and up to his face. He looks angry, like a demon, as he stares straight ahead.

I exhale and ask, "Why did you do that?"

"Do what?"

"Hurt that black guy…" I ask, immediately regretting my question.

He lets out a laugh, throwing his head back. His laughter startles me, but I try my best to hide it. "Why not?"

"What did he do to deserve that, Dad?"

My father turns, glaring at me. "Are you questioning me, boy?"

"I just want to know," my voice breaks. The fear increases because I know I've shown weakness.

"He was born, son! That's what he did." My father grinds his teeth as a smirk appears. "He's a black bastard and living off the system, while I have been a hard-working son of a bitch my entire life. What do I get for it? Nothing!"

The movie stops playing, and it is just McIntosh, his colleagues, and me. I gasp for air and shake my head. "That was when I saw true evil for the first time. I'd learned later that guy died in the street. I caught in on the morning news. I watched with my father. He seemed unphased by it all. The guy was found the next afternoon. People thought he was a passed out drunk or something. A little kid found him," I say, pressing my teeth together to keep myself from crying. "I also learned that he didn't owe my father anything. My father hurt him because he could. Because the man was black."

McIntosh makes a few notes. I see him glance over at the others, who give him a nod. He looks at me. "I am sure that was very traumatic, James. It gave me chills just listening to your story. I can tell it has shaken you as well, but this is good. This is actually very good. We need to keep this going. So, you claim what your father did to be true evil, correct?" I nod and he asks, "How did that true evil shape you?"

"What do you mean?"

"Did you ever commit an act of violence towards a person of different race or color?"

His question causes a knot in my stomach. Not just because of the subject, but because the answer is filled with an ugly truth. I run my hands over my face and a breath escapes me. "Yes."

"Care to tell me... well, us... about it, James?"

"I don't know if I can," I reply. My voice is filled with the weakness I know my father hated. The weakness I was beaten for.

"Yes, you can, James. Yes, you can," McIntosh says, almost like a mantra.

I hear Abel telling me no, but before I know it, the truth is pouring out. "It was in college. I shared a dorm with an African American guy. He was a few years younger than me, and he looked up to me. He wanted to do everything that I was doing. I had lost my grandfather a few months prior, so I was into some bad shit."

"What sort of bad shit, James?" McIntosh enquires, causing me to dig even deeper into my past.

"I was drinking, smoking weed, and taking pills. Not in that particular order either," I reply. "So, one night a few of my other buddies from class want to get together. My roommate wanted to come. I warned him that they were a bunch of rough and rowdy white boys, which they were. He wanted to go either way, so I brought him, against my better judgment."

"Did something happen to this young man that you speak of?"

I nod. "Yes. He was severely beaten."

"By the other boys?" I nod. McIntosh makes a few more notes before looking at me. "And I'm sure you felt guilty over that. Would I be correct in assuming that?" I nod once again. He scribbles some then leans forward in his chair. "Unless you participated. Did you, James? Did you help beat that young man?"

"No, I didn't beat him. All I did was watch. I didn't do anything to try to stop it. I just watched."

"Well, did you take him to the hospital or call 911?"

I shake my head. "No. I left him there. I stayed until I couldn't take anymore. I left, and they weren't finished yet." I exhale and look at McIntosh. "I never saw him again. I only know what I saw and from what I read in the newspaper after he was found."

"Were you ever questioned about it?"

"Yes. I told the police that I left to go pick up another friend. I used the text I got from one of the guys, saying it was over, as a way to tell the cops why I didn't go back, because I figured the party was over. I told them I didn't know anything about what happened."

"But you did, James."

"I know." I close my eyes as the memory arrives. I relive it, just standing there in the dark next to a fire as my roommate is beaten left and right. I can hear the insults as well as his cries for help. I open my eyes. "I could have done more. I should have done more."

"Why do you think you didn't, James?"

"I'm not sure."

"I believe," McIntosh says as he leans back, "it is because you have a fascination with others being hurt. You grew up in a world of violence, therefore violence became your world. You take a fighter, for example. You step into a ring or a cage, and you fight for your life. Like them, you need violence. For you, it is kill or be killed, because that was the way it seemed to be with your father."

"But I don't want to hurt others. I don't want to see others hurt. That isn't who I am."

"That is all for today, James. Thank you for meeting with me. I think we took a step in the right direction," McIntosh says before getting up from his seat. He walks out of the room, and his colleagues disappear from behind the glass. A few orderlies walk in, escorting me out of the room. We make our way through the workout area McIntosh had mentioned during my first day. Seeing a group of African American men talking and lifting weights makes me weak at the knees due to the content of my therapy session, so I keep my head down, not wanting anyone to see the guilt on my face.

20

I am led to my cell in X6, where I stand lifeless for a few moments, wishing I didn't have to relive the memories I just shared with McIntosh. I know people usually feel a weight lifted off their shoulders, but I feel like I'm being crushed. I lie on my bed when I hear Abel's voice.

"You are so damned dumb, James." I sit up and see him pacing back and forth in the cell, looking at me every so often. "You are letting McIntosh win. Does that not make sense?"

"I'm not letting anyone win, Abel. Hell, you weren't even there, so you don't get to come in here and pass judgment on me," I sneer.

"What you just did…" Abel shakes his head. "What you just did… it gives McIntosh even more reason to keep us in here. I don't know about you, but I'd rather not spend the rest of my days in this fucking place. I would assume you feel the same way."

"You know that I do, but I came here to get rid of you. To get rid of whatever demons I've kept harbored in my head."

Abel fades, but another voice chimes in from behind me. "I know all about demons."

It was my neighbor, the best friend-killing psychotic. He looks at me. The crazed look in his eyes appears to be frozen as he continues, "I can't get the demons out of my head. My best friend, his family… I see them all the time. They visit me here when I'm awake. I see them when I'm asleep. It seems like you talk to yours…." he gives a light chuckle. "And you said you weren't insane."

"I'm not," I fire back. "I'm nothing like you."

Another chuckle. "Not yet," He says, before turning away from me. His words chill me to the bone to the point where I can't question him. I return to my bed, curling up into a little ball, telling myself that Abel isn't right, that the lunatic beside me isn't right. I shake my head, telling myself that I am going to get out of X6. That I will leave Trinity. That I'm not beyond saving. That I won't die here.

21

I'm walking through a field. Flames burn high and bright on both sides of me. I can feel the heat. It feels as though I can barely breathe. I keep moving.

Because I see him toward the end of the field.

Waiting for me.

Quentin.

He looks alive and healthy, as far as I can tell. This becomes more apparent the closer I get. The crunching underneath my feet catches his attention as he turns to me. His eyes are dark and hollow.

"What took you so long?" he asks as I stand before him. I want to hug him. To do anything just to see if it's real.

I try, but I can't for some reason.

"What are you talking about?" I ask in response. "I'm here now."

He turns from me, and I can see his wounds slowly appear.

"You weren't here when I needed you to be."

I look down. "I wanted to be. I wished I could have been, Quentin. Not a day has gone by that I've not thought of you, and I can't describe to you the blame I've placed on myself."

"You always want to be there for people, and yet you're never there." He looks at me, part of his face young and smooth, the rest of it beaten it and battered, covered in rotting flesh.

"I do the best I can."

"Do you?"

"What the hell do you want from me?"

"You weren't there for your siblings. Logan and Holly. They needed you when they were younger," he states as he begins walk slowly, forming a circle around me. Flames follow him with each step he takes.

I shake my head. "No, no. I tried my best to be there for them. We were kids. I could only do but so much," I cry out, memories of the beatings they received when I wasn't good enough for my parents racing through my mind.

"Look what your best did for them," he says, as some flames part, revealing an image of my sister. She no longer looks youthful. She looks sickly. Long gone are the days where everyone praised for how beautiful she was. And I can't look away, no matter how much it pains me.

I watch her as she cuts.

The blade pierces her skin, tearing through it as blood sprays from the wound. Her tears fall at first, but the more she cuts, the less she cries.

The flames consume her. She looks numb as she bleeds.

"Why are you showing me this?"

More flames go out, showing my brother. He no longer looks like a star athlete. He looks worse than my sister. Blisters riddle his limbs, even the fingers gripping the needle. I watch as he tightens the belt around his arm, slapping it as he searches for the perfect veins. He plunges the needle into his left arm, into a black hole that looks as rotten as Quentin's face.

"Stop. Stop. Stop!" I shout, and the image lingers a little longer, before going up in flames. I turn to Quentin, as his flesh continues to rot. "Why did you show me that?"

"You were supposed to protect them. You couldn't. You were too weak to do so. Now look at them. Their lives have gone to shit, and it's because of you, James."

I shake my head, feeling tears beginning to build

"This is why they want nothing to do with you."

"You don't know what you're talking about it."

"Oh, but I do," he states joyfully. "They want nothing to do with you because you're a constant reminder of the pain they had to endure. Of how much you failed to protect them."

I drop to my knees, a rage rising within me. I shout into the flames. I shout at him.

He laughs. "And when I really think about it, you couldn't have protected me. You couldn't have done anything for me. I'm better off dead." He howls with laughter, throwing his head back as I watch the flames consume him.

"I wanted to, Quentin. I truly did. I wanted to protect Logan and Holly. I'd love nothing more than to see you all again. Alive and healthy. Just the way I want to always remember you."

My words seem to fall on deaf ears, as he continues to laugh, as he continues to burn. And then, he just stops.

Still on my knees, I look up at him. What was left of Quentin is no longer there. I can only hear his voice.

"You've failed everyone, James. Those you love and care for. Even yourself. You belong at Trinity."

"No!" I shout, shaking my head. "I'm going to leave here. I'll be better."

"I know you really don't believe that. You belong at Trinity, where you can suffer for your failures."

I wipe away tears streaming down my face. "I've suffered enough."

He laughs again before lunging at me. Leaping on top of me, he holds me down. I struggle, but I can't break free.

"You've not suffered nearly enough, James. Not nearly enough. You deserve to be burn like me."

I continue to struggle, but it's no use. All I can do is let the flames consume me as they have Quentin.

The fire grips my clothes, and I can feel my flesh burning. I cry out, but nothing stops it. The flames continue to rise, and there's nothing I can do.

I can only accept what's going to happen.

22

"Tell us, James…" McIntosh pauses before flipping through my file as we sit in the interrogation room, his colleagues on the other side of the glass once again. "Do you have a name for your violent side?"

"You know that I do," I reply.

He frowns. "Well, tell us his name, if you don't mind."

I search the room to see if Abel is around. He steps out from behind me, looking at me as I try not to make it obvious that I'm looking at him too. Abel shakes his head no. McIntosh's voice chimes in my ear, "James? Are you still with us?"

I nod. "Please," he says, "tell us the name of your violent side."

I glance down, looking away from everyone, including Abel. "His name is…" I let out a deep sigh, "Abel."

McIntosh nods as well. "Alright. Can you tell me the most recent act of violence this…Abel…has committed?" He finishes the question, looking up from his notepad and looks at me.

"An act of violence that I remember, or the one you told me I committed?"

"The act you're able to remember, James," the good doctor sternly states.

I draw in a deep breath and hold it, letting the memory return. I exhale, "I attacked a co-worker. I slammed him face first into the concrete floor, breaking his nose in several places. There was blood everywhere. Abel did that. When I got back into the driver's seat, I saw what I had done, and I knew I had to get away from everyone."

He jots down notes, as do his colleagues. "Alright. Thank you, James. Now," McIntosh begins, "do you believe you can tell me the earliest act of violence where Abel was in control? I know you spoke about the bully in the bathroom, but you said you only saw flashes. Was there ever a moment where you knew Abel was in control and he did something violent…something that you saw and remember?"

"I remember the first time I saw Abel face to face," I say, no longer seeing Abel in the room. "My siblings and I had been sent to LA, to stay with other family. This was due to my parents' ongoing drug abuse, and the fact that they needed a break from us. My aunt was a foster parent. She had a girl staying with her. This girl and I didn't seem to get along all that great, until one night…" the memory plays out before me, "a guy got a little hand-sy. He didn't seem to understand the concept behind the word 'no.' I didn't like that and neither did Abel. I let him do whatever he wanted to the guy."

"I see. And how did that make you feel?"

I shrug. "It was one of the few good things Abel did."

"And you said, that was the first time you saw him face to face. What does he look like?"

"Like me. There are scars covering his face," I say.

He writes a little more, and I become curious as to what he is really writing. His pen stops moving, and McIntosh looks at my file for a few moments before saying, "He has scars on his face. According to these notes, the scars have gotten worse. Is that correct?" I nod, and he asks, "Why do you think that is?"

"I believe they became worse over the years because Abel's actions became worse," I say.

"I see." He nods and scribbles more. "What do you believe to be one of worst things Abel has ever done?"

I squirm in my seat. "I'd rather not get into that, Doc."

"But we need to, James!" he snaps at me before taking a quick breath, as if he is simmering down. Once the breath escapes him, he flashes a grin and carries on like nothing happened. "We had this discussion the other day. You have to confront this in order to move forward," he reminds me.

I run my hands over my face and my head, letting out a growl. "Fine," I say, grinding my teeth together. "Abel used to stalk women. He wanted to hurt them. When I had a girlfriend, he would take over when we were having sex. It would be rough and violent. But if you really want to know…" I pause, shaking my head. Memories of Kerri, the woman Abel threatened because she was nice to me, flood my brain. As well as the sex with an ex-girlfriend, Julia. Abel felt she was using me, and in the end, she was, but during our relationship, he wanted to punish her. And then, the last memory, the worst of all, rises to the surface.

I see it as I tell him. I tell him about Eliza, my daughter's mother. I tell her how we met years ago and lived the rock-and-roll lifestyle, complete with the sex and drugs. I tell him how things didn't pan out, despite having a daughter. I tell him how she and I decided to be friends, and how she had another man in her life when Abel was at his worst.

"Abel broke into Eliza's apartment," I say, trying not to choke on my words. "He snuck into her bedroom." I can see her. Her black hair, pale skin, dark eyes as she rests on her bed. What I say next causes the sickness to rise from the pit of my stomach. "Abel took pictures of her as she slept. Eliza used to always sleep in the nude…" My voice breaks as I shake my head, trying to rid myself of the memory, but it continues to haunt. "And then, Abel decided to pay a visit to my daughter's room." I stop and look down.

McIntosh writes furiously until he says, "Go on, James. You can do this."

23

Ah, this city... the smog and pollution... breathing it in through my nostrils lets me know that I am right when it comes to the way I view the world, the way I urge Sir James Evans to view it and its moronic inhabitants. They ruin everything. Everything they touch seems to turn to shit. James has learned this. Well, at least I hope that he has during his many attempts to BLEND IN and be like the lot of them.

It made me sick to see him to do so. The fact that he even let such an idea slip into this brain of ours made me want to vomit. He hates it even if it takes him a while to admit it. That is why he has me. I am here to guide him and nurture him.

Just as I am right now, my hands on the wheel and my foot on the gas. I am in control. James tries to keep me cooped up, and it is driving me... well, us... insane. Now that James is asleep, I doubt he will have any issue with me using the body to go around and have my kicks, satisfy my needs. Man, if only that Kerri bitch lived in New York, I'd pay her visit and have my way with her. It wouldn't even matter if she was willing or not. I am, and that's all that matters. I want to have some fun. I need to have some fun. And what do I mean by fun? Oh, I mean to hurt someone in some way, shape, or form. So many of these morons these days love to go out and drink or smoke. No, not me. Poor James did it but he did it to shut me up. He did it to fight the urges to do what he truly wants to do.

No matter. I am here now, and I know that sooner rather than later, little James will come around and give in to his true nature. He and I will finally be one. But until then, I will have to take over from time to time. Works for me. With the way James is right now, all torn and shit, he would more than likely slow me down and I can't have that. I can't be cock blocked when I'm about to ravage some poor defenseless street walker, and by ravage, I mean... kill. Ooohh... just thinking about it gets me off.

This city... such a vast disappointment.

People living off social media. People doing all that they can to look, and live, like their favorite celebrities.

Ah yes, I know what James is thinking. We view the world the same way. We think the same way, but enough about us. I want to have some fun. So, what do I want to do first? Hmmm, let's see…I'll go for a run. It gets the blood flowing. I take another look up at the big screen before feeling my legs moving, gaining speed with each step growing into more of a stride. I am sure I look funny to anyone who pays attention as I am wearing all black with the hood of my jacket pulled over my head, allowing it to cover most of my face. But this is New York, Abel, I remind myself, therefore nobody is paying one bit of fucking attention.

Knowing this causes my grin to grow.

I pick up the pace when I see a couple walking together, hand in hand. I know that James would hate seeing this just as much as I do. I feel like he and I are of the same mind when it comes to women. Fucking them is the only best course of action. If you must play the game in order to do so then so be it, but don't play too long because I am pretty sure James learned with that Eliza cunt that there is no pussy worth playing games for.

But there are some games that I like…

Such as running up behind an unsuspecting person and clubbing him in the back of the head. The man drops to one knee after I put almost the full of force of my weight into the elbow. Before he can get up, I shove my foot into the side of his face. His lady goes to scream but I backhand, putting all my weight into it. I watch as she spins around and collides with the concrete wall beside of her. Her boy toy grabs me and tries to wrestle with me, which I can't help but laugh at before driving my elbow into his groin. He drops again, but I hold him up a little, my gloved hands—smart, I know—gripping his shirt collar. I then drive my knee into his ribs once, twice, three times for good measure. I take a moment to smile at my handiwork. I look over and I see a few cops running towards me, hands on their guns I presume. They are yelling at me to stop as I put my feet to pavement and run off into the night, laughing it up and enjoying just how much damn fun that was.

I continue to run, not really looking to slow down since I am sure that the cops will be looking for me. I know that I will have to think fast about where I need to go. I could go back home but I am not quite ready for that. That doesn't seem as fun. Hm…I wonder if Eliza is home. Oh… I like that idea. I stick to the shadows as much as possible as I make my way through this slum of a city, harassing a few people here and there, mainly the homeless as well as a prostitute I plan on coming to visit later.

I run until I reach Eliza's apartment. I keep my hood up, and I take a few moments to sit on the front steps of the complex to catch my breath. And I need to wait for someone to step outside of the building so I can slip inside. I sit there, clapping my hands together, enjoying the moment, and feeling the rush of life. I don't know why James doesn't embrace this way of life. It's much more fun. Ah, no matter. As I said, he will come around. And then the door opens. I quickly stand up as a gorgeous blonde walks by me.

I get the impulse to bend her over the steps before passionately sodomizing her, but I don't. I slip inside of the building and I recount my steps, remembering where Eliza's apartment is. I've been here before with James so I tell myself it shouldn't be that difficult. I go up some steps then come to her door. I continue to walk by it, however, keeping my head low with the hood pulled over my face, because I noticed the security cameras on the way in. They have some on every floor. I stand in a corner and I watch as the camera moves slowly, gathering up information on the floor, and I begin to time it. I watch it a few times before picking up its pattern and then I spring into action, quickly but quietly picking the lock. I glance at the camera out of the corner of my eye and see that it is coming towards me again, so I stop what I'm doing and head back down to the corner, letting the camera do its thing once again.

I watch as it turns away from me, away from Eliza's door, and then I sprint down the hall to finish what I started. I ease the door open, then pull out the little magnet that James picked up years ago. It comes in the shape of a pen, so it is easy to use. I pull the chain back before easing the door open the rest of the way and slowly, quietly closing it behind me just as the camera scans by.

Once inside, I feel a grin spread across my face. I then take a deep breath before tip-toeing down the hallway, looking at all the pictures hanging on the walls. I see a few photos of Eliza and her other kids Sadie and Sarah, James' daughter Sophie, and some guy that Eliza is fucking.

Lucky bastard.

I stare at it… NO… I fucking glare at it, grinding the teeth James and I share, as I lift the picture off the wall. I feel the anger rising in this vessel as I take the opposite fist and punch the picture, cracking the glass before hanging it back on the wall. I then turn and head down the hallway a little more before coming to a door. It is cracked a little and I can see Eliza as she sleeps. I grab hold of the door and push it ever so gently to make sure it doesn't make any noise. Once inside of the room, I stand above her, the once-love of James' life.

I lean my head down and slowly sniff her, gliding the nose from her ankle up her silky-smooth thigh. I stop at her vagina and I hover above it. I feel its warmth radiating on my face. The urge to have my way with her begins to jitter all through my body. I want to work my fingers and tongue before ramming my throbbing cock inside of her, wet or not. I bet James would love the way she feels especially when she is crying and afraid, our hand over her mouth to muffle her screams.

I stand up quickly as her body moves. She then lies on her side, the covers drawing up a little. I see her back and her ass. She is wearing black see-through panties. Oh, she shouldn't have… I remove James' phone and take a quick souvenir.

I then slowly back out of the room, pulling the door back to where it was before looking at the other room where the children sleep. I stare at them, as I remember how having a child makes James soft, how he gushes over her and loves her.

Just the very thought makes me sick. It is things like these… these children that can really hurt James in so many ways. They can hinder him. Just a few days ago, he took them out for dinner and ice cream. He was all nice and sweet towards them, even Eliza, even though she stabbed him in the back years ago. It would be so easy. I chuckle at the thought. It'd be so easy to just remove them out of James' life permanently. I look over and see one of Sophie's pillows resting on the floor.

I lean down and pick it up before looking at Sophie. Sweet and innocent, so easy to do….

I grip the pillow on both sides as I slowly step towards her bed until I am next to her bed, hovering above her. I hold the pillow in front of my chest, above her head as I remind myself of how easy it would be to…

24

"Abel grabbed a pillow and decided to smother my daughter in her sleep," I say, a heavy sigh breaking free of my lungs as I picture myself standing in Sophie's room, a pillow gripped in both hands as I edge closer to Sophie, seeing her resting peacefully. "He got closer. The pillow was above her face and then," I gasp for air, trying not to relive it, "I stepped back into the driver's seat," I say, before turning my head to the right, letting the sickness escape. Orderlies start to come into the room, but McIntosh waves them off. He and I lock eyes as he motions for me to continue, his eyes showing some excitement. I take a few deep breaths before sitting up in my seat, trying my best to regain my composure. "I saw what I was doing, and I left the apartment as fast as I could. I didn't know it at first. I had woken up the next morning, thinking it was nothing more than a bad dream. I remember how panicked I was…"

"I called Eliza," I continue, "and everything seemed fine. I went over there as soon as I could to see them, as if I needed to protect them."

"When did you know it wasn't a dream?"

"I checked my phone. I saw the pictures of Eliza. I went to her apartment. I saw a picture Abel had cracked. I saw my daughter's pillow in the same spot I had left it."

He writes a little more before saying, "So, Abel wanted to murder your daughter."

"I've always believed that was what he wanted," I say, trying to fight back tears as well as more sickness. "That's why I went to Vaughn. I couldn't put my family at risk."

"Commendable," McIntosh says before setting his notepad to the side. He crosses his arms and legs as he stares at me, as if he is looking inside of my soul as well as what is on the other side. "Would you like to know what I think, James?"

"I don't know. I feel ill," I say, not enjoying the trip down memory lane. "I want out of this room. I want to go back to my cell. I don't want to do this anymore."

"While I understand, James...I can't say that I sympathize with your situation, son. You see, I believe you're a very violent person. I have no doubt that you see Abel as the one committing these violent acts, but I believe Abel wanted to hurt those people, wanted to hurt your daughter, because you wanted to."

"What the fuck are you talking about?" I ask, slamming my fist down on the table, "I would never want to hurt my child. She is my daughter, you asshole!"

He doesn't flinch. "I know she is your daughter, but I am sure that you wanted to hurt those women for various reasons. Kerri, you say she was nice to you, and Abel became infatuated with her. She rejected you, I'm assuming," I nod, confused as to where he is going with this. "So, that pissed you off. You wanted her to pay, because in your mind she had to be with you and no one else. When this Julia that you spoke came into your life, she used you. You wanted to use her. You wanted to be one step ahead of her, and when you couldn't, you wanted to hurt her as well, to establish some sort of dominance."

I shake my head. "No..." I feel weak. "You're wrong."

"And you said that Eliza, the mother of your child, was with another man after things didn't pan out between the two of you," he continues. "You probably saw it as her being happy while you weren't. You were being used and rejected. She couldn't be happy then."

"Stop..."

McIntosh doesn't stop. "And when it comes to your daughter," I feel my hands form into fists, my veins beginning to pump madness into my body, mixing a cocktail for destruction, "she had been, at that time, the only thing keeping you somewhat sane, if you want to call it that. You prefer to be violent, so deep down, you wanted to get rid of the one thing keeping you from being who you truly are."

"No!" I shout, bolting from my chair and slamming both fists on the table before flipping it over. I see red as I take a step toward McIntosh, who is now behind his own chair, trying to keep it between us. "Oh, you want to talk your shit, but you don't want to deal with the consequences?"

Orderlies enter the room as McIntosh tells them to stand down. He looks at me. His expression enlivened. "And what would the consequences be, James?"

I look at the orderlies then back at him as I say, "Send your dogs out and I will fucking show you. You do not talk about my daughter like that."

I stand tense, keeping my fists up, not letting them shake unlike the rest of my body, which quivers with rage. McIntosh and I keep our eyes locked as I see a smirk appear on his face. "Take him back to his cell. We're done for now."

The orderlies circle around me before moving in to grab me. I do my best to wrestle away from them, as I want to hurt McIntosh in the worst way, but they prove to be too much. I see McIntosh for a moment before I feel a needle dig into my neck. I keep my eyes on him for that brief moment until my world turns to black once again, with his overly arrogant smirk being the last damn thing that I see.

As everything remains black, a clanging soon enters my ear. It sounds very close, and it gets closer, causing my eyes to open. I find myself back in my cell. The clanging continues. I turn around, realizing I'm in my bed, and I see Lance standing outside of my cell. I slowly sit up, my head throbbing as usual. "What do you want, Lance?"

Lance looks around before looking at me again. "You're letting McIntosh win, James."

I close my eyes, squeezing them shut, and it keeps the pain at bay. "I've been told that before. I've not figured out what it means. So," I say, opening my eyes, "tell me what it means, Lance. You seem to be happy as shit here at Trinity, so tell me how you make it work."

"I don't fight him, James. You're fighting him. You're fighting the system."

I get out of my bed, stumbling a bit before collapsing into the bars. "All he has done is feed me with pills, stab in the damned neck with a syringe...shooting God knows what into my body."

"He wouldn't do that if you didn't fight him, James. Fighting him lets him win. He gets to do what he feels to be best when it comes to your behavior," Lance says.

I shake my head. "Lance, he wants me to act out or become violent. He triggers it, so he can use me as some sort of goddamn experiment."

Now Lance shakes his head. "No, James. He is trying to teach you how to control it. He is going to keep doing what he does until you learn to control your anger. Until you learn to rid yourself of the violent personality." Lance looks around again. "McIntosh likes to give us pills. It keeps him in business. He does it to help you...me...all of us."

"You have no damned clue what you're talking about, Lance," I say, shoving myself away from the bars. "You're a lunatic. Just like he is. If I don't fight him, then he wins. I can't let him win. I have to figure out how to beat him and his system." I exhale. "I have to figure out how to get out of Trinity," I say, waiting for a response, but I get nothing. I slowly turn to see not Lance, but an orderly standing there. "What is it? You going to tell on me for talking to Lance? Go ahead, and do your worst."

The orderly shakes his head. "No clue what you're talking about, James. I'm here to see if you'd like to talk to your wife. She's come to visit."

My mouth hangs open for a few moments as I try to process what he said. "How did she know where I was?" I ask, knowing she couldn't know about Trinity, as I didn't know about it until I arrived here.

The orderly shrugs. "I don't know, James. All I know is that she is here. Do you want to see her or not?"

Before I can say or do anything, I hear McIntosh's voice. "Is there an issue?"

I glare at McIntosh as he walks toward my cell. "Yeah, there is an issue. I want to know why my wife is here when she didn't know I was coming to Trinity."

McIntosh steps closer to the bars. "She is here because I reached out to her, James. Your outburst earlier today was yet another setback. I felt the need to contact your wife because I have this hope she can get through to you."

I stand before him. Lance and Abel's words of me letting McIntosh win run through my head like cars during the Daytona 500. I take a deep breath, trying to calm myself as I say, "My wife does keep me sane, but that doesn't give you the right to try to use her as some sort of pawn in whatever game you're trying to play here."

"I assure you that none of this is a game," McIntosh says with a shake of his head. "This is for you, as I want what is best for you, James."

I press my face against the bars. "She's what is best for me, and I don't want her to be part of this. I don't want her to come to see me, especially when you've called her."

He throws his hands up in surrender. "That is fair, James. There is only one thing that I feel needs to be mentioned."

I get a sense of dread that I try to mask, letting it shoot up and down my spine but nowhere near my face. "I figured as much. More damned games. Alright, McIntosh. What is it?"

He lowers his hands as he steps away from my cell. "You cannot discuss anything that occurs during your time here, while you are still a patient. Therefore, Braelynn cannot be told of anything that you've experienced here. It would be a breach of confidentiality."

I roll my eyes. "So, you're asking me to lie to my wife? You bring her here because you feel she can get through to me, but she has no idea what is going on? You want me to be all rainbows and fucking smiles?" I shake my head, sniffling a little as I step away from the bars. I repeat his statements to myself before charging back to the edge of the cell, locking eyes with McIntosh. "You know...you're the one," I say, pointing at him, "you're the one who should be in here."

McIntosh frowns. "That's the thing, James. I'm not in there. I run this place, while people like you fill it, giving it life, feeding my purpose in this world. There is one other thing you need to consider, James."

"And what might that be?" I ask, feeling beyond tired of playing this game, despite what he continues to say.

"You need to figure out what you want your purpose in this world is, or what it can be," McIntosh replies.

I want to punch him in the face. I want to rip out one of his eyes and force it down his throat. That is how sick of McIntosh I've become in such a short period. I don't know if that is Abel slipping into the driver's seat, or if it is my own personal thoughts and feelings. But I say nothing in regard to harming him. I swallow it all before exhaling, "Take me to my wife."

25

Braelynn enters the comic shop in black skinny jeans, black flats, and a gray Captain Marvel shirt. I look up from my Spawn comic as Sophie drops her Spider-Man book and races towards her. "Brae-Brae!" Braelynn smiles at Sophie as she bends down and scoops her up into a hug. Braelynn kisses the top of my daughter's head as Sophie seems to be hugging my girlfriend as tightly as she can, "I missed missed missed you, Braelynn," I hear Sophie say. Her words make me smile, telling me that I am definitely making the right decision, especially with my little bit's approval.

"Is that so," Braelynn asks as she adjusts Sophie on her hip. Sophie smiles and nods her head as Braelynn continues to speak, "Well, what if I told you that I missed missed missed missed you bunches? Would you believe me?" Sophie grins as she taps her chin as if she is processing what Braelynn said. She then stares at Braelynn and just grins. Braelynn appears shocked, "You better believe me, woman, because it is so true. I missed missed missed missed you," Braelynn states before proceeding to hug and tickle Sophie as the comic shop fills with laughter.

I make my way over, "Alright you two. You are disturbing the peace," I say as I take Sophie in my arms. I kiss her on the forehead before placing her down, "Go finish reading your book. Find some good stuff so we can read it when you come over. Alright?" I say, and Sophie nods before heading off. I watch as she goes. Braelynn steps beside me and I say, "I'm glad you dressed appropriately for my favorite place that has now become your favorite place," I state with a slight snicker, which results in me getting a gentle punch in the arm.

"Hey, you brought me here. Remember that?" Braelynn says, shooting me a sarcastic look, "So what are you two up to? I didn't know you were going to get her today. I would have gone with you to pick her up. It would have been awesome to see Eliza."

I look at Braelynn, "You don't think it's weird to see my ex-baby mama?" Braelynn shakes her head no and looks at me like I should already know the answer to my question. "I'm sure I wouldn't want to see your ex-baby daddy if you had one. I'd feel so..." I try to hide my grin, "inadequate... or something?"

Braelynn rolls her eyes and shakes her head, "You are so full of shit. You know that?" I nod my head incessantly as she continues. "Besides, if anyone is going to be my baby daddy... something tells me it'll be you," she says, giving me a wink before making her way over to the shelves and grabbing at a few of the new Marvel titles. "So, what brought you guys out here today? I figured you would have been sick of this place by now with how much I've had to drag you here," Braelynn states, shooting me an evil grin.

I fumble with the ring in my pocket, trying to fight back the urge to break out into a nervous sweat and hives. I take a deep breath before I respond, reminding myself that I am making the right decision. I replay what Sophie said, and this brings me a sense of ease and comfort, "Well, I wanted to give you something. It's a surprise, actually. It's something Sophie, and I picked out. I should probably mention that since I'd feel guilty for taking all the credit."

Curiosity fills her eyes as she tries to hide her already forming smile, "You got me a surprise? You have so got to stop doing that, babe. You know don't have to get me anything."

I playfully cut her off, "Well if that's the case, I guess I could take it back," I say with a slight shrug.

She grabs my shirt collar and pulls me close, "I did not say that, now did I?" She asks before giving me a kiss on the cheek.

"I don't know. You told me that I didn't need to get to you anything. I mean, to me... it just seems like you don't want it," I say, giving her a wink. She balls up her fist at me and I throw my arms up to shield myself, "Oh God please don't hurt me. I'm fragile..." I state in a whimpering voice.

Braelynn sighs, "Okay, now I know you really are full of shit."

I nod. "Guilty. Guilty as charged."

"So, what is this surprise you have for me?" Braelynn asks.

I shrug. "Well, I can't tell you, but..." I say, motioning to the left with my eyes, "if you really want to know then you're going to have to go around to the back of the store, to the last set of bookshelves. Once you get there, you will find what you're looking for. Do you think you can handle it?"

She looks towards the back of the store then back at me and nods confidently. "I think I can handle it. In fact," Braelynn says as she flashes a smirk, "challenge accepted."

I nod in approval. "Live long and prosper," She nods as well before I watch Braelynn heads towards the back. A few of my fellow nerdy brethren check her out as she makes her way to the back. I don't get jealous because I know in my heart of hearts that she is going to be mine. Oh yes, she will be mine. I take a few moments to gather myself as I slowly pull the ring out of my pocket, following her by keeping my distance so she doesn't notice me, and then I find her standing above Sophie, who looks up at her smile. I take a knee as Sophie motions for Braelynn to turn around.

She does just as I pop the box open. We lock eyes, and she begins to cry and smile. Braelynn wipes her eyes as I ask, "Will you..."

I don't get to finish as she bursts out, "Yes, yes... Yes!"

I grin, "I'll take it," and I slide the ring onto her finger. I kiss her hand then look up at her. "So I guess this means you love me even more, right?"

She smiles and says, "I do."

26

The cell doors open, and I step out only for the orderly to step before me with handcuffs. I look at him then at McIntosh. "Are you fucking kidding me? Handcuffs? I'm not a fucking criminal."

McIntosh shrugs. "Well, you are in X6. It's where we house our most dangerous patients. We are taking you across the grounds, James. We can't have anything happen. You're quite the risky endeavor, if I do say so myself."

I let the orderly place me in handcuffs, snapping them around my wrists as well as my ankles as I keep my eyes on McIntosh. "I've been across the grounds since being in here once before. There were no handcuffs involved then. What is the difference now?"

McIntosh grins. "I changed my mind. You being in handcuffs makes me feel a little safer today."

I feel my teeth press down against one another, moving back and forth, bone against bone as I say, "When I get out of here, I am going to make sure this entire place burns."

McIntosh leans forward and whispers in my ear, "If...you get out of here." And then, I hear a soft chuckle echo in my head. The desire to hurt McIntosh intensifies. I feel it ricocheting against my teeth, rattling in my bones, but I do nothing. He steps back. "Now, would you like to see your wife?" I give a nod, and he says, "Wonderful news. Keep in mind what I said and enjoy your visit. We will have another therapy session once your visit is complete, just to see if it helped. I will see you shortly." And with that, McIntosh walks away, disappearing from my view.

The orderly leads me out of X6, which is a bit of a struggle due to the restraints. They have them extra tight, as if I have committed murder. I feel like Hannibal Lecter minus the mask. I don't think I would actually eat the flesh of another human. The very thought of eating a human organ makes me queasy. There is a chance that I would bite someone and rip the flesh from their face or something along those lines, but to ingest it completely...I pause, shaking my head, wondering why those thoughts were even crossing my mind.

We cross the grounds, entering the building known as X3, which is where the patients are able to enjoy recreational activities such as TV and weight training. The orderly removes the restraints once we enter, then he leads me upstairs and down a hallway. We reach another room, where tables and chairs are spread throughout, reminding me of the college cafeteria that I went to four or five times before the incident with my old roommate. I see his face, reliving the beating he received before it all fades as my eyes rest upon my wife's face.

As she does with any room, she lights it up. Seeing her generates a warmth in my body I've not felt since leaving her just a few days ago. I walk into the room and take two steps before she is rushing towards me, wrapping her arms around me. It feels like forever since I've held her close. Feeling her body against mine, feeling her heart beating against mine, I don't want to let her go. I don't want to let her leave without me. Feeling her lips press against my cheek, I feel alive again. Braelynn rests her forehead against mine. As we stand in this moment, I feel a glimmer of happiness, of hope. I tell myself she is why I am doing this, as I don't want to disappoint her and hurt her in any way.

Our embrace ends, and we walk hand in hand over to the table where she sat when I first saw her. We sit across from one another, and she continues to beam. I continue to fake it. Braelynn clutches my hands in hers as they rest in the center of the table. "I've missed you so much, James. I can't put into words how I've felt since Dr. McIntosh called me to have a visit with you. He seems to genuinely care about you," she states reassuringly.

All I can do is nod, despite the part of me that wants to laugh at the very thought of McIntosh giving a damn about me. "You really think so?" I ask, part of me thinking that if Braelynn can believe it then maybe I can, too. That maybe this truly is all in my head. That after this visit, I can get with the program, follow McIntosh's lead and get my mind right, before having him thank me for coming as he sends me home.

Braelynn nods as well. "Yes, I do. I really do. He told me that you were having a tough time, but he didn't get into any specifics. He felt that getting to see me would shake you out of whatever funk you've been in."

I force a smile. "He said all of that, did he?" She grins excitedly. I look at her for a few moments before leaning closer. "Things aren't what they seem to be, babe," I say in a whisper. I look around, hoping no one can hear me before facing her and continuing, "McIntosh isn't what he appears to be. The way he talks, the way he presents himself…" I pause, taking another look around, feeling like all eyes are on me. "It is a lie. It's a fucking facade."

Her smile fades as Braelynn looks around as well, a slight panic in her eyes. "What do you mean?"

"He's not here to help me or anyone else in here. He's toying with our minds. I just don't know how. But," I say, glancing to my left and right, "I am going to figure it out. I have to. Not only for myself, but for everyone else in here. There's no telling what sort of damage he has caused."

Before anything else can be said, orderlies surround us. McIntosh steps in from behind him. He looks at us. "I'm afraid I'm going to have to cut this visit short."

Braelynn looks at me. The panic in her eyes has heightened. "Why? Is something wrong?"

McIntosh nods, "I'm afraid so." He then turns to me, "James, I thought this visit would help, but it appears it has only increased the delusions in your mind. I am going to need you to come with us," he says sternly.

I look at my wife. Seeing the worry on her face eats at me. I rise to my feet, feeling a tingling in my fingers, knowing that I am going to regret what I am about to do. I lock eyes with McIntosh, and I nod before driving my forehead into the bridge of his nose, hitting him as hard as I can. He staggers back. The surrounding noise dials down as I begin fighting with the orderlies. I can see McIntosh grabbing at his bloodied nose, pointing and barking orders at the orderlies as other patients and their families cower away. I keep fighting, swinging for anyone and anything as they all try to wrestle me down to the floor. I sink my teeth into an orderly's ear. I hear no screams as I grind, the taste of flesh, the metallic taste of blood consumes my mouth and throat, before a sound enters the room.

It is my wife's voice as she shouts my name. I go limp, keeping my eyes on her as she stands at the table. The orderlies all grab and swing at me, but all I focus on is her and her voice as she continues shouting my name.

"James!"

I blink, and I'm sitting across from her. She is still holding my hands in hers. I look around. Everyone else is carrying on conversations. There are no orderlies. No McIntosh. I look back at my wife and I can tell she is worried. All I can think about is the hallucination I just experienced. All I can think about is how mad I'm going. How I am just like my neighbor in X6.

I'm going insane.

27

"Are you alright, babe?" Braelynn asks, gripping my hands as tight as she can. I look down at our hands. They are so perfect together. They fit and look complete until I slowly pull them away. She tries to maintain her grip, but my hands are able to escape hers.

I look into her eyes as the worry becomes something else. I just can't tell what it is. I force another smile. "Thank you, babe. I'm glad you came. I'm even happier I got to see you, but you can't come here again."

She goes to speak, but I get up from the table, turning away and heading for the door. Once I reach the door, the orderly opens it, but I stop. I look at her as she looks at me. I can see what her worry has become. It's become sadness. I give her another nod before stepping out of the room. As I follow the orderly down the hallway, I catch a quick glance of Braelynn as she begins to cry before burying her face in her hands, and I curse myself.

I curse myself as I'm placed in restraints once again. I curse myself as we cross the grounds, returning to X6. I curse myself as the restraints are removed and I step back into my cell, still cursing. I picture Braelynn's sadness as it fell from her eyes, before calling myself a fucking bastard.

"I came here to get better," I say under my breath, "but I've done nothing except make things worse."

I sigh, burying my hands in my face. I want to keep my face there, cupped in my hands, hoping to smother myself somehow. I visualize doing so before glimpsing into the future. Sophie and Braelynn are devastated. I go further. I see Sophie going to high school, getting her first car for graduation. I see Eliza and

Braelynn waving her off with teary smiles as she heads off to college. My face cupped in my hands, I actually smile, a few tears of my own striking my palm.

I see Braelynn meeting someone. He has a good job and a good family. He gives her everything I want to but can't. They smile and laugh a lot. They get married and raise a family.

"You're letting them win," I hear. I bring my face from my hands, expecting Abel or Lance, but instead I see my neighbor, smiling at me, flashing his teeth at me, rotten like the rest of him.

"Who are you?" I ask, wiping the tears from my eyes.

"The name is William Jones. I thought you recognized me. I guess no one talks about me anymore," he says, giving a sad face before quickly throwing his head back and laughing. He then looks at me. "I shouldn't be sad. I had my time in the limelight. I was famous for quite some time."

"How long have you been at Trinity?"

"Too long, friend. Too long," William wheezes.

"We're not friends," I state quickly.

"But we can be. Especially with you being in here. It helps to talk to people just like you." He gives a snicker. "Otherwise, you'll go crazier than you already are."

I go to say I'm not crazy, but I can't find the strength to say it. I just shake my head. "Shut up," I say, turning away from him.

This doesn't stop William. "You really are letting them win."

"I don't know what the hell that means. It seems everyone who tells me that...they have their own definition."

"Waging war against yourself," William cackles, "always generates different results. Or voices. At some point, one will stick, and you'll follow through. I had many voices. The one that told me to kill my best friend and his family...it seemed to fit. It all made sense, so I followed what it said. Everything in my life made sense."

"I don't want to follow a voice in my head. I want to get out of here," I snap back.

"McIntosh, this entire fucking place...nothing is what it seems. You're letting them talk circles around you."

I scramble across the cell to the point where only the bars separate us. William grins wickedly the closer I get. "What did you say?"

"You're letting them talk circles around you."

I shake my head. "No. Before that."

"Nothing is what it seems."

I nod rapidly. "Yes, that! What do you mean? You must know something."

"Oh, I do. I know many, many things. When I came here, I wasn't like this," William says, looking himself over. "The food they serve, the pills they give us...there is something in all of it that causes our brains to change in ways we would never expect."

I shake my head, trying to process what he's saying, "What do you mean? You're saying they put things in the food and the pills? What sort of things? How does it change our brains?"

He nods. "Oh yes! They put things, a little bit of this and a little bit of that, but no one knows for sure. All I know is that I've killed three people since I came here. They ended up putting me in X6, and McIntosh has left me here to rot."

Hearing his words, I create some distance between us. "You've killed since you've been here? Jesus fucking Christ," I say, exhaling deeply. "No wonder they've left you to rot. You're a damned monster."

"The thing is," William starts, "I don't remember murdering anyone except for my best friend and his family. McIntosh has only told me that I've killed. I don't have a single memory of it. I've never remembered any of it. All I know is they've continued feeding me with pills. There are days I've forgotten. Entire fucking days!" William shouts, rising to his feet, and shaking the bars like some sort of wild animal.

I stand as well. "William...William...stop...stop," I say, looking around, hoping to calm him down. He looks at me. "Listen to me, friend..."

William cuts me off, "Friend? Friend? We're friends? I thought you said we weren't?"

I shake my head, "That was before I realized we've so much in common," I say, not believing the words as I speak them. "There have been things I can't remember. I've been told memory loss is one of the side effects from the medication they've given me."

"Have you killed anyone?"

"No," I say, "but McIntosh said I've attacked patients and orderlies. I've had images running through my mind of hurting people. I contemplated eating organs and human flesh when I left my cell earlier. That isn't something I would normally do."

"It's the pills and the food! I'm telling you the truth, James!" William exclaims.

"I need to figure out what they're giving us. The only thing I can figure out is that whatever it is, it is designed to make us more aggressive." I shake my head once again. "He said he wanted to cure me of my violence. It seems he wants to do the exact opposite."

"We can't let them win…." William says, his eyes pleading. "We can't let them win."

I nod. "I know. I know. I'm going to try, William."

28

"Hey James," I hear another voice call out from behind me. William's eyes fill with worry as he shuffles away from the bars. I turn to find Jeffrey standing at my cell. "It's time for therapy. Let's go," he says, raising restraints up to the side of his head.

I step out of the cell and he puts the restraints on, snapping them tightly around my wrists and ankles once again. I follow him across the grounds, expecting to go into the interrogation room, but we take a detour. Jeffrey opens a door that leads to a stairwell. He looks at me. "This way, please."

"Where the hell are we going?" I ask, speaking for the first time the entire trip.

"Dr. McIntosh decided to move therapy elsewhere. He feels it will be good for you," Jeffrey says, as nicely as he can.

"I don't like this," I reply, taking a step back. "I'd like to go back to my cell."

"Unfortunately," Jeffrey says, his calm demeanor becoming something I've never seen from him, something sinister, "that isn't an option, James. Especially if you want your journal."

"I'll get my journal?" I ask, recalling the reason I've wanted it, in order to keep my thoughts and memories collected just in case I lose time again.

Jeffrey's look changes again, becoming more upbeat. "Oh yes, I've spoken with Dr. McIntosh and he feels your journal could be a positive. He just wants you to attend this session and you'll get it."

Against my better judgment, I follow Jeffrey. We make our descent, and we walk down a lightly colored hallway with a black door. He opens it and I step inside. The room is black as well. I see a chair and Jeffrey motions for me to sit.

I do, and before I know it, he has used the restraints to strap me to the chair. I struggle a bit, but I can't move.

"What the hell is this?" I ask, trying to break free once again.

Jeffrey steps into the doorway as Dr. McIntosh enters the room. He says, "It's therapy, James. It is the same thing we do every single day. This shouldn't come as some sort of surprise."

"I can't say I've been tied to a chair for any therapy session we've had," I fire back.

"It shouldn't be any different from any other day for you, James."

"What the hell does that mean?"

McIntosh breaths over his glass lenses, then wipes them down as he says, "You've kept yourself restrained for a very long time. You won't give in to your aggressive personality."

"I thought you wanted to cure me of my violence."

McIntosh chuckles, "I'm going to assume you believed that. James, I know you've talked with William. We have eyes and ears everywhere here. I figured you would have realized that from the get-go."

"What the fuck do you want from me?" I hiss.

"I WANT..." he shouts, before drawing a deep breath, pressing his hand to chest as he appears to calm himself, "... to bring out this aggressive side of yours. You're aggressive by nature. You just choose to keep it hidden. You know what you're truly capable of, but you fear it. This world is ruled by the mentality of kill or be killed."

"And yet you keep people like William here?"

McIntosh shakes his head. "William is the way he is because he stayed with me before. I brought out his aggressive nature, his true self. He embraced it, killed people he cared about, and got caught."

"So what? You're creating monsters and priding yourself on that shit? Go fuck yourself, Doc!"

"No. Monsters only exist in fiction. My work...what I'm doing is purely science. I'm bringing out the worst in people. Once I do that, I study them, learning all I can while observing and collecting data. With that data," he continues, sounding nothing less than thrilled, "I come up with ways to manipulate those violent personalities in the best ways possible. You came here because you are weak, but within you, I see untapped potential," McIntosh says, taking a step closer to me, dropping to eye level.

"I'm not letting you out of here until your true self comes out. And I'm not talking about some part time bullshit. No, I want it to live freely."

I try to move, trying to headbutt McIntosh, but the more I struggle, the tighter the restraints become. "You have no idea what you're doing, McIntosh. I don't want to be violent. I don't want voices in my head. I want out of here."

"I told you how that would work. No more games. William let the cat out of the bag, but hey...what can you do?" He chuckles, "You want out? Stop being weak. It is kill or be killed. Kill that weak side of yourself."

"I'm not weak," I hiss once more, "You're weak for trying to pull this bullshit. I will beat you, McIntosh. I know what the monster inside is capable of. I know what he can do and what he has wanted to do. I've beaten that before, and I can do it again."

McIntosh grows quiet, rises, and takes a step back. He looks down, defeated. "You're right, James. You've beaten the voices in your head before." And then, he looks at me. "Or have you?"

"Yes, I have."

"At least, that is what I've wanted you to think, James."

"What...what do you..." I can't finish my question, as a memory returns. I see me as a kid, resting on a couch. A man towering over me with a syringe. I see my eyes open as the syringe pierces my skin. I see a man. It is Dr. McIntosh.

29

"What did you do to me?" I ask McIntosh, no longer struggling in my chair, feeling defeated.

"We can discuss that at a later time. We need to begin your therapy," McIntosh states he steps back into the hallway for a few moments. When he returns, he has a group of African American patients. The same patients I saw after I disclosed what I saw my father did when I was younger. After I disclosed what I did in college.

"What is this?"

"This is therapy, James. I've already told you. I've told these fine gentlemen what your father did, as well as what you did in college. Actually, I've told them what you didn't do," McIntosh says, "And, I think in order for you to get rid of your weaker self, you need to be cleansed of your sins. Once you do that, you will be able to move forward, letting go of the guilt of the past."

I say nothing, knowing what to expect. The patients line up in front of me. One by one, they begin hitting me in the face, the stomach, anywhere and everywhere. The beating doesn't stop there, as they circle me, each taking a shot. It doesn't take long before I taste the metallic tang of my own blood. I taste the flesh off one of their knuckles as it meets my teeth, bone against bone. Soon, the beating stops.

McIntosh steps forward. "Alright James. Tell me, do you still feel weak? Or do you want to get up and fight back? You would make your father proud. Your college buddies would cheer you on."

I spit out blood. "Fuck you."

McIntosh nods. "Suit yourself." He motions with his fingers, and the beating continues. I see a fist flying towards me. I feel pain for a moment, but only for a moment. The room, the patients, and McIntosh fade.

I find myself in a mosh pit of violence. It is filled with people I've hurt in the past. I see Eliza. I see Kerri. I see Julia. I see countless faces. They are all swarming me. Hitting me, beating me down to the ground. Every single time I try to move, I am kicked in my ribs, but I keep pushing myself to my feet.

I get to my feet and I begin fighting back, swinging at anything and everything. Telling myself that I can't let them win. That I have to fight back. I swing, connecting with bone, feeling their blood spray across my face, before I managed to break through the crowd. They all begin to follow me as I realize I am in X6.

They chase me and I fight back, swinging and knocking some of them down before running some more. They do not stop. They remain resilient. But I tell myself I must fight back. I challenge them, and they keep fighting, making me pay for my sins, but I tell myself my sins cannot define me. I have to keep fighting. I fight for myself, and for those I love. I have to fight the ugliness of my past, so I swing with all I have.

I feel a hand grip my shoulder. I am spun around. I see my face, except with scars. It is Abel. He grips the back of my neck. He pulls me close, as I look around confused. Those I've hurt, my past sins all stop, forming a circle around Abel and I. He kisses the side of my face, before I feel a sharp pain ripping through my flesh, tearing into my abdomen. I gasp for air as Abel speaks, "Hush...hush now..."

I step back, reaching down to find a knife sticking out of my stomach. I drop to my knees. Those I've hurt, my past sins all begin rushing towards me. They begin hitting me, as life slowly starts to slip away. Abel drops down to one knee as the violence continues. He brushes my head, as if he is trying to provide me with comfort. I want to scream and cry, but nothing happens. I'm able to tell myself one thing, and I repeat it.

I deserve this.

I deserve this.

30

I fall to the side, and as I hit the ground, I am no longer in X6. Abel isn't around. I am back in the same room with McIntosh and the patients. McIntosh is kneeling before me as I rest on the floor. The patients kick me and hurl insults in my direction.

"Do you want to fight back?" McIntosh asks, brushing the side of my head. "Do you want to fight back? Just say the word and I will tell them to stop. You will be able to have your revenge. You can hurt them as they have hurt you."

They continue beating on me, but I feel nothing. I can only see their feet colliding with various parts of my body. I look back at McIntosh who asks again, "Do you want to fight back? James, you can stop this. Let this weak part of yourself die. I will nurse your violent side back to full health. He will be stronger than ever before. You can let go of that past guilt. You can grow from this. He...can grow from this."

I spit out more blood. "I deserve this."

McIntosh sighs and nods his head before rising to his feet. He takes another look down at me before shaking his head. I watch as he exits the room, closing the door behind him. The beating continues. I do nothing except lay here, visualizing all of those I've hurt, all my past sins, and I repeat to myself that I deserve this.

I deserve this.

I deserve...

31

I hear a flick, flick, flicking followed by the smell of something burning. I open my eyes to find my father staring down at me. I blink a few times as everything becomes clear. I see the white walls, with holes in them from meeting my father's fists. I look to my left and I see the fireplace. I see a spot of blood in the exact spot where my head connected all those years ago.

I finally look back at my father as he pulls his burning cigarette from his lips, snapping his lighter shut, exhaling. And then, he looks at me. His face is worn and tattered. He looks twenty years older than he should be, thanks to years of hard drug use, not to mention the abundance of alcohol he consumed on a daily basis.

I know my father is dead, but he looks as real as ever.

His eyes, the color matching mine, stare at me as he runs his left thumb and index finger through the mixed blonde and gray whiskers of his mustache, "I always knew you would end up in some mess you couldn't get out of. I knew you'd always be afraid of who you really were. Of you who you were always destined to be."

I manage slowly pushing myself to my feet, my body aching like I've had a month-long flu virus. The bones throb with each shift of my limbs. "And who was I destined to be?"

My father, Franklin Evans, chuckles as he shakes his head before taking another drag of his cigarette. "You are my son. You remember me as a violent bastard. I didn't take shit from anyone. If I wanted something, you know that I took it. Just as you know that I never cared about hurting anyone, no matter who it was, in order to get what I wanted."

"How could I forget?" I ask, shuffling closer to him. "I've got plenty of bumps, bruises, and scars to remind me just how much you never cared about hurting someone."

My father rolls his eyes, places the cigarette between his lips, visibly cracked, as he plays an imaginary violin to mock me as only he would. "Are you still singing that same song? You know that you could have stopped me at any time, James. Yet you didn't."

"You were my father…"

He shrugs. "So what? I could always see the rage inside of you. Some of the shit that I did, I did just to provoke you." Another drag, and another deep exhale as the smoke hovers around me. "I know you could have put me through a fucking wall whenever you felt like it. I know you could have. You just didn't do it. Because you're a coward. Afraid of your own goddamn shadow."

I feel my hands tense. I want to strangle him. I want to hurt him, just as I wanted to hurt him when I was younger. Just as I have always wanted to hurt him.

Abel's voice rings in my ears once again, "James, stop. You'll let him win."

I shake my head, "I've let everyone at Trinity fucking win! What difference does it make?!"

My father manages to chuckle despite my hands around his throat. "Exactly, boy! It doesn't matter. Give into it. Kill me. Do what you've always wanted to do!"

Abel pulls me away, throwing me to the floor. I land next to the blood spot. I look at it, overwhelmed by how real it looks. I touch it. It's still warm, like the so-called accident from my childhood had just happened. I look at Abel as he towers above me. "Why did you do that?"

"Because Abel is going soft," I hear my father say between gasps and laughter. "You're both losing your edge. Christ!"

I scramble to my feet, fuming at Abel. "Are you trying to be the noble one now?"

Abel sighs, "I've told you before. You're different, therefore I'm different too. I was against going to Trinity. That never changed. But I know you want to be a good person. If you go through with what that monster wants you to do, then there would be no going back. You will have crossed the point of no return, James."

"Maybe I need to," I reply. As soon as the words escape my mouth, I glance down, feeling shame. I run my hands over my face, letting out a sigh of my own. "Maybe I should just do it. Maybe I need to give McIntosh and everyone else what they want. What they expect."

I hear my father laugh again, but I don't engage.

Abel replies, "And why do you think you need to do that?"

"Are you my shrink now?" I ask, keeping my eyes to the ground.

"Just answer the damn question, James!" he fires back. I recognize the frustration in his voice.

My gaze meets his, "Because it'd be easier. It would end all of this. McIntosh said if I gave into the violence then I could go home. I could be with my family again."

Abel shakes his head now. "That man has done nothing but lie to you since you arrived. You are nothing more than a guinea pig. That is all you have ever been, James."

Before I can say anything, my father stumbles in between us, shoving Abel back then grabbing me by the throat, giving me no time to react. "You're not going to let that fucking weasel ruin this! You need to do this! Let that violence out! Breathe it! Be..." my father fumbles through his coat before his free hand emerges with a gun. He places it in my hand, cocks it before he points it to his own head as he wheezes, "... it...."

He squeezes my throat as I feel my finger grazing the trigger, and then, Abel speaks as he gets to his feet, "James... Don't!"

"Will you shut the hell up?" my father bellows, rolling his eyes before looking at me. "Don't listen to him. Listen to me. I know how bad you want this. Just do it. I want you to do it, I want you to do it. Make me proud, son. Come on!"

I yell, wrestling away from my father, shoving him back. Abel catches him before my father jerks away. Both look at me. I see them then stare at the gun resting in my shaky hand. I tell myself that I need to do this. That I have to do this.

I place the gun to my head. My father and Abel shout at me, but their words become inaudible. I feel the cold of the steel as it presses against my skin. I think of my wife and daughter. All that I will leave behind. I tell myself that they wouldn't suffer due to my own suffering if I do this.

I take a deep breath then squeeze the trigger.

There is a loud bang.

32

I open my eyes to find myself in another room. There are no signs of Abel or my father. I rise to my feet, my head feeling like scrambled eggs. I look around, trying to recognize my surroundings, but I can't. This is a room I've never been in, or even seen.

There is another loud bang. Pain jogs through my skull. A pain that reminds me of my return home after one of my first therapy sessions as a child. The pain was always in my head. I recall this just as my brain produces the memory of Dr. McIntosh standing above me as I rested on his couch all those years ago.

I see the needle breaking the skin.

I close my eyes, trying to block it out. Another bang, followed by a deafening scream this time. I open my eyes, taking the room in.

The room is wall to wall concrete. The floor is concrete. The walls and floor have portions missing, as if someone or some people had been chipping away, trying to write a message, trying to convey how they felt.

Everything looks dark green and slimy, like the room gets plunged into a swamp on an hourly basis each day. There is a bed but given the dampness of the skin on my face, I can tell I have never made it to the bed.

How long have I been in here?

The situation with my father and Abel was nothing more than a hallucination, I tell myself. It is more than likely a side effect of yet another pill that McIntosh put into my system. I shake my head, laughing at myself as I say that I'm nothing more than a walking medicine cabinet.

Just say no, James.

I snicker as I recall my mother's words when it came to drug use. She would tell me to never be like my father, to never let my life turn into the mess he had made hers.

Of course, she would tell me this right before heating the bottom of a spoon and shooting up as I sat on the couch with her, watching her fade away as my siblings watched their Saturday morning cartoons.

I should have said no to my father, I think to myself.

Even if it was a hallucination, why did I turn the gun on myself? Do I really want to end things? Do I really want to give into McIntosh and what he wants? The thoughts make me ill. I remember reading long ago how hallucinations can be the mind's way of forcing you to deal with things you've buried, or things you choose to ignore.

Is giving in the right thing? Am I ignoring that? Is it even remotely true? I press the middle of my forehead against the damp slime of the wall, gently bashing my skull into it over and over, as the questions do the same to my mind.

And then, I hear a lock unsnap as the door to my recently discovered new home begins to open.

McIntosh steps inside the room, followed by two orderlies. He looks at me for a few moments before motioning to them. The orderlies step closer to me, and before I know it, I am shackled to the floor, chains around my hands and feet. I am too weak to fight, so I don't try. There is no struggle. Just acceptance.

The orderlies step out of the room. I look at McIntosh as he towers over me, just as Abel did in the hallucination.

"Where am I?" I ask, my voice nearly hoarse.

"Solitary," he says, running his hands over his beard and adjusting his glasses.

"Why?"

"I figured you needed time to think, James," McIntosh says as he drops to one knee. He looks me over, studying me like I am a piece of art. "Goodness, James. They really did a number on you. You took quite the beating, my friend. But," he says with a snort, "it didn't have to be that way. You could have fought back. I would have made them stop. You could have returned the favor."

I swallow, though there is nothing to swallow. Just the air I breathe, causing my throat to dry even more. "I'm not some sort of monster," I sigh. "Why are you doing this? Why the fucking mind games? You've lied to me since I arrived here."

McIntosh sighs as well. "James," his next statement breathes a little life into me, "I've lied to you since the day we met. I've fed you lies since you first came to my office many years ago."

My mind quickly recalls the image of him standing above me. My eyes closed as I rest on the couch. The needle.

"How long have you known me?"

"I can't recall how old you were, James. I think you were a teen, or close to it. You told me your life story, and I knew you would be a perfect candidate."

I grind my teeth together. "Perfect candidate? What the hell are you talking about?"

McIntosh chuckles and shakes his head. "James, people say that mental health doesn't get the attention it needs or deserves, but that is very far from the truth. You see, the government pays very close attention. They are always watching, James. It is very much Big Brother, despite what many civilians think or feel."

I feel a fight rising within me, but I know there is no use. The chains keep me at bay. All I can do is bore holes through him as McIntosh continues, "They look at certain people. People like your father, who was always into crime, even at a young age. He had such a violent nature. That kind that the government loves to exploit."

My teeth grind harder. "Just tell me."

McIntosh exhales, "James, I need you to hear the full story so you can get a better idea. I need you to see the big picture."

"Fuck you, you sick fuck!" I shout, using what little fight that had built up.

He removes his glasses, breathing onto the lenses, and cleaning them with a handkerchief he removes from his pants pocket. "I was hired to work with your father, but I realized how much of a waste he'd be. His years of hard drug use really destroyed what could have been. And since he decided to keep all the drugs for himself, your mother provided us with a unique opportunity in order to get her next fix."

"Don't you talk about my mother!" I hiss, just as I did in the hallucination, shouting at the ghost of my father. "My father was a damned monster. My mother wasn't."

McIntosh tilts his head slightly to the right. "Are you sure about that?"

116

33

My body shakes with anger as I want to beat McIntosh within an inch of his life. I want to beat on him until my arms get tired. I curse the chains. "You're lucky these are keeping me from getting to you. If I could, I would hurt you. I swear to God I'd hurt you. My mother was a good woman. My father destroyed her…"

A sliver of laughter exits his lungs. "Oh James, if that is what you truly believe then maybe you're not the greatest of candidates."

My chest moves up and down at a rapid pace as I struggle to gain my bearings. "What do you mean? Stop playing games, God damn it!"

"First," McIntosh says as calm as can be, "do you remember anything about me from your childhood?"

My breathing slows slightly. "I remember," I say as the image returns, coming alive in my head, "you are standing above me, telling me to go to sleep. I remember you standing above me, a syringe in your hand. I remember the needle moving closer toward me before sleep fully took over."

McIntosh nods. "Ah, that is perfect, James. That was the first time I experimented on you. Just remember, it wasn't my idea. Everyone has a boss who gives orders. I had orders to follow. But yes, your mother came to me a day or two prior, asking me to give her some medication, anything to make her numb for a little bit. She needed a fix, James, and she needed it badly."

"What did you do?"

McIntosh removes a handkerchief out of his pant pocket then takes the glasses off his face. "I offered her a solution, James. I only wanted to help," he says as he breathes onto his lenses, then begins to clean them with the handkerchief. "I needed another subject. I asked her if she had any children with any mental health issues. I told her if she did then there was a chance that I could help her with her needs." He replaces the handkerchief and the glasses back in their original spots and grins as he looks at me. "She gave you up without a second's hesitation, James.

"She told me of your trauma. You had been through a lot up to that point. Your mind was already capable of creating voices. It was able to generate a violent nature within you. My experiments only accelerated the inevitable. I turned in my notes to my employer, and they loved you. You were the perfect candidate, James. You should take some pride in that."

I flex my muscles, feeling everything ripple as the anger courses through my body, hoping that I can somehow break the chains binding me, keeping me from him, as he adds insult to injury. "Your mother...what a saint," McIntosh says as he begins to laugh.

I strain, trying to break free. "You shut up! You shut the hell up! Lies! It's all lies!"

McIntosh steps closer. "Oh, I wish it was, but sadly, James...it's not. What I've just told you is the honest to God truth."

Hissing through my teeth, I reply, "Why should I believe a single fucking word? You've lied to me every step of the way."

He shakes his head. "I told you the night I gave you a choice... the truth. I opened up to you, just as you needed to open up to me, to let that violence run free. That violent nature that I toyed with and accelerated...since you were merely a boy. The medicine I had been provided with by our lovely United States government didn't work with everyone, but it worked with a select few. Including you."

"So, you're making monsters? That's what I figured," I say with a scoff. "You sound like a fucking comic book," I state, hurling spit in his direction.

"Monsters? No, James. We are making man stronger, because in this life, in this world, it is survival of the fittest as well as the smartest. The government owns pharmaceutical companies, James. Companies you've heard of, as well as some you haven't. And not just in the U.S. People believe Canada to be nothing more than a bunch of pussies, but when you dig a little deeper, you realize they are far darker than we are."

He continues, "They pay people like me, building facilities like this, selecting only the strongest," he giggles, "but the pay aside, I took this job because I love the way the mind works. I love the way I can manipulate it and make the mind work the way I want, just a little more."

"What do you, and those who pay you, want?"

McIntosh smirks, "To unleash upon the weak. My employers want those who survive this process, who become one with their violent nature, to turn on those who allow themselves to be beaten down by society on a consistent basis. By ridding the world of its weak links, there is a chance the world could return to a perfect harmony. It would be a return to our own little Wonderland."

I cringe when he says the world. I see him grin, "I see that word still cuts you."

"What are you talking about?"

"Your siblings were watching Alice in Wonderland. They were with your mother in the living room." As he says it, my mind conjures up the memory. I see my siblings sitting on the floor, eating cereal. It's a Saturday, and just as McIntosh stated, they are watching Alice in Wonderland.

I step closer into the memory, only to see my mother on the couch. She is overdosing. I rush over to her. A younger me. I can tell by the look in my eyes that I am beyond panicked. I shake her and slap her, begging her to be okay, and one word escapes her mouth. "Wonderland."

The memory fades and I see McIntosh kneeling before me, closer than he has been before arriving in this room, my solitary concrete Hell. "It's funny how that still triggers you, James." He is close enough, so I do it. I drive my head into the bridge of his nose. He falls back as blood pour from his nostrils. He looks down at his hands as they pull away from his nose. He sees the blood. He coughs as he climbs to his feet. I can tell by the look in his eyes that he panicked a little. "You will pay for that, I'm afraid."

"Fuck you," I growl.

McIntosh knocks on the door and it opens. He gives me one last look before stepping out. I hear him say, "Have some fun." He steps out of sight as the orderlies step inside, bringing the door to a close. I look at them, knowing there is nowhere to run. All I can do is accept what is coming. When I feel the first kick to the face, I tell myself the pain is worth it because I was able to hurt him.

34

My face is puffy from the beating I received, but I manage to see through slits where my eyes are nearly swollen shut. It hurts to breathe through my nose, but I pull myself off the floor. My body throbs, finding little comfort in the semi-soft mattress in the corner of my concrete tomb. I pull my knees up to my chest, hoping to sleep through the pain, but instead I hear Abel's voice from behind me.

"So, now you know the truth," he says, letting out a sigh.

"Did you know what my mother did, Abel?"

Another sigh. "Yes, I did."

"Why didn't you tell me? This entire time I thought my father was the monster…"

Abel cuts me off before I can continue. "He was a monster, James. There is no denying that. He turned your mother is a junkie. He made her into exactly what he wanted. He wanted her to share his misery."

"Why did you keep it hidden from me, Abel?" I ask, my face roaring with agony. Everything aches and becomes worse each time I speak. "Had I known how long McIntosh had been involved in my life, things may have been different."

Abel replies, "Do you think so? How do you know you wouldn't have run to him like you did? I didn't tell you, James, because you didn't want to know. I didn't show you the full memory because you wanted to keep that shit buried as deep as possible."

I manage to roll myself over so I can face Abel. He looks at me. The expression on his scarred face is a combination of remorse and disgust. "James, why did you let them do that to you?"

My lips move, forming a half grin as I reply, "I thought you were supposed to be the violent one. I thought you were supposed to be the one to fight back. Where were you?"

Abel shakes his head. "That isn't how it works, James. Either the meds they've been feeding you have kept me away, or you're blocking me out. Had I been able to, I would have taken that beating for you, James. I would gladly stay in the driver's seat until the pain went away."

I groan, slowly sitting upright. "It doesn't matter at this point, Abel. I'm not getting out of here. McIntosh enjoys using me as a guinea pig. I mean, shit... he's apparently done it for most of my life. Why would he stop now?"

Abel looks down, shaking his head. "What?" I ask.

He exhales heavily. "There is a way to get out of here. But it's not what you want to do, James. That's the thing."

As soon as he says it, I know what Abel means. I know I'd have to give McIntosh what he wants. I know that it would result in more collateral damage to those in my life, to those waiting for me outside of these walls.

"James?" Abel asks, but I say nothing. I turn away, feeling as defeated as I'm sure I look, before lying back down, knowing what I have to do. The very thought eats at me.

It eats away at my flesh like a cancer, ripping life from me. Thoughts are the most dangerous things, as thoughts become ideas, and ideas become reality.

Just like the people McIntosh is associated with had thoughts. They have a vision of the way the world should be. That vision, those thoughts, generated idea after idea, and someone finally put their foot down before those ideas were put into action, making them a reality. I am living fucking proof, I tell myself, grinding my aching teeth together, swallowing the blood leaking from my busted-up gums.

Just as William is living proof. I wonder how many patients have been used as guinea pigs. We are all rats in a maze, with McIntosh controlling the twists and turns, getting off on us having to bend beyond our means.

William has been a pawn just as I am. Just as they want us to be.

Days pass by slowly in this concrete tomb. No sign of sunshine and nighttime. Every day is the exact same. My wounds heal. I push my body to work through the pain, doing push-ups and sit-ups. Anything to keep my muscles tight, pushing my endurance, as all I have is time. I rebuild my strength. I push and push, building myself brick by brick, before I find myself beating on the door to my unwanted Fortress of Solitude.

I shout for McIntosh. I shout with all that I have, with my voice going my hoarse as my throat turns raw.

I lose track of time. I don't know how long I have done this for. Calling out for McIntosh feels futile at times but I continue, even during my workouts, using my hatred for him as motivation.

And then, the door finally opens. I am in the middle of another set of push-ups. As the door comes open and light shines into my tomb, I quickly scramble to my feet, telling myself a beating could happen at any time. And then, stepping out from the light I lock eyes with Jeffrey.

He gives me his carefree smile. "How are you, James?"

I suck sweat and snot as I shake my head, lacking the desire to play games. "Where he is?"

"Who, James?"

"McIntosh," I growl. "I want to see him."

Jeffrey nods. "I see. Well, I will see what I can do."

"Cut the shit, Jeff! I know you sons of bitches have heard me. I know the Good Doctor has heard me. I have yelled, screamed, and begged for him for only God knows how long. He's heard me. I know he has. I want to see him," I say, stepping closer, standing just inches from Jeffrey, "and I want to see him now. If he wants to get what he wants out of me, then he will grace me with his fucking presence," I hiss.

Jeffrey maintains his smile, "Dr. McIntosh will be delighted to hear you have said that. I will let him know," he states gleefully before stepping out and closing the door, leaving me shrouded in darkness once again.

35

I lose track of the time once again, never knowing when it is day or when it's night. For all I know, I tell myself, it could be the same day. It is just that the hours feel longer. But it feels as if time stops when my door opens again. It's Jeffrey, as well as two more orderlies. I rise to my feet, my face not throbbing as much as it had been.

Jeffrey says, "Dr. McIntosh will see you now."

I walk forward, lifting my hands as handcuffs are wrapped around my wrists and ankles. It's all protocol. A safety precaution. I am sure my file states I've become a hazard to my own health. A danger to those around me, I tell myself as I visualize McIntosh jotting those words down in his notes to make me look as insane as he wants me to be.

This is his world, I tell myself. He is God here, which I am sure he gets off on. The idea of playing God. I came here to be fixed. If I want to leave, I will have to take McIntosh's cure, whatever concoction that he's designed to meet the specific needs of mine that he wants to exploit in some way.

I shake my head as we journey through the halls. The halls echo with the screams of patients who are also locked in solitary. My brothers in soon-to-be insanity, I'm sure. The sun shines through the windows, blinding me at first. It takes a bit for my eyes to get adjusted. I have grown so accustomed to my concrete tomb that everything looks brand new, like I am in a foreign land.

"How are you feeling today, James?" Jeffrey asks.

"Just take me to McIntosh."

"Very well."

I'm sorry, Braelynn, I tell myself as we continue walking. I should have listened to you, I say as I visualize my wife walking in front of me, glancing at me every so often over her shoulder. I can see a look of worry in her eyes. Seeing those eyes in person could save me, I tell myself. I should have let her save me as she has saved me since the day we met.

I'm sorry, I tell her. I want to reach out to touch her, but I know I can't. For once, I know this isn't real, but despite that realization, she looks as real as ever. Visualizing her, I realize just how much I need my wife.

Her words repeat in my head, "Are you sure you want to do this?"

I curse myself, wishing I had stayed home. Home. The thought of being home sends chills down my spine. I look at Braelynn, telling her that I am going to do what I must do in order to return home to her. To my daughter. So we can be a family. A real family, without all the bad wiring I have going up in my head.

"Alright, James?" I hear my name, causing the vision of Braelynn to fade, leaving me more haunted than the hallways of Trinity have been believed to be. I look to find Jeffrey staring at me. We are outside of McIntosh's office.

I swallow sickness and sadness, tasting the worry in my sweat. "Yeah, I'm fine. I'm ready to get this over with."

"You don't look so good," he says.

I shake my head. "No, I'm fine. We're here. Let me talk to him."

Jeffrey knocks as I am pressed against the wall by the other orderlies. The door opens, and it doesn't take long for my eyes to lock in on McIntosh, like a shark smelling blood in the water. "Hello, James. I've heard you've been asking to see me. Is that true?" I nod profusely, fighting the urge in my mind and body to wrap the chains binding me around his throat. He smiles. "Are you sure you're up to it? You look ill."

My voice sounds like grinding gravel. "I've been in solitary for only God knows how long. The food hasn't been that great," I say barely recalling a proper meal during my time in my tomb. "I've not slept great... so yeah," I say with an arrogant sneer. "I don't have any doubts about how ill I look."

McIntosh nods. "No reason to be hostile, James. I'm just trying to assess you. I want you to be okay, as I've said in the past."

I shake my head. "No games, McIntosh. I'm not biting, so don't bullshit me. I've not forgotten what you told me. That's why I'm here."

"I see." He looks at Jeffrey and nods. I am led into his office and restrained to a chair. I hear McIntosh tell them to standby on the outside before closing the door and taking a seat at his desk. Placing his elbows on the desk, his fingertips rub against the hair on his neck and chin. "So, are you sure you understand why you're here?"

I nod. "Yes. I want to get out of here. I will do whatever I have to do to get out so I can be with my family again."

"You were very much against it before, James. Why the sudden change of heart? I'm curious, because like you, I don't want to play games. Not at this stage. I do not and I will not. So," he says before getting up from his seat, walking to the front of the desk, crossing his arms over his chest, "I will ask again. Are you sure you understand…?"

I cut him off, "Just fucking tell me what I have to do, and I will do it." I look down, feeling my stomach churn. My chest fills with pain after uttering the words. I tell myself that it will be for the best but trying to comfort myself does nothing of the sort.

"You will have to give yourself to me, James. And by that, I mean your mind," McIntosh states, pointing to the side of his head. "Once we cross this line, there will be no going back. Your most violent side will come to the surface and will become my instrument."

Cocking an eyebrow, I ask, "Instrument for what?"

"My instrument for success," he says. "I've never had a patient become truly successful in this process. People like William… as I said, he was a failure. He wasn't able to balance the violence with regular everyday life. I feel I've tinkered enough with the formula to make it work. If you go this route, then I will know for sure."

"And how will you know?"

McIntosh chuckles, throwing his head back in the process. "Oh, James! You want me to give away all my secrets. I thought you said you understood what you were doing?" He makes a pouty face. "Do you…do you not trust me?" he asks mockingly.

I hesitate to respond, waiting for Abel to show his face, to linger in my ear so he can talk me out of this, but nothing happens. He doesn't appear. There is only silence. I exhale, "I have no reason to trust you. I've been a guinea pig. Your guinea pig. You've fucked my life up, so what's one more way to do so. I just want to go home and if I have to do this…" I choke on my words a bit before clearing my throat, "if I have to do this… if I have to let you win in order to go home…" My next statement weakly escapes, "Then, so be it."

"Delightful," he says before returning to the other side of his desk. He begins to fumble through the drawers before his hand emerges with a pill bottle. He shakes it at me, laughing with glee. He pops the top and a green pill slips into the palm of his hand. "Are you sure you want to do this?" Hearing him ask reminds me of Braelynn and how I should have said no. Just as I should say no to him. I simply nod, but he shakes his head. "I need a definite yes or no."

"Yes!" I shout, feeling so tired, so drained, so weak from all of this. "Yes... yes... I'm sure," I say looking down, trying to hide my shame as I ask, "What is that, though? I need to know what it is."

I see McIntosh walking towards me, the pill in his hand, as his voice echoes in my head, "The key to your freedom."

Freedom, I tell myself.

A chance to go home.

To be with my family.

The one thing I want more than anything else.

36

I'm all smiles. I have been brought out of X6, where I say goodbye to William. I walk into the main building. Before I know it, I am surrounded by nursing staff. They are all clapping for me, praising me, celebrating what I have done.

What have I done?

I've been cured. I did what I needed to do to leave Trinity. To return to society. And most importantly, return to my family.

I shake hands with Dr. McIntosh, the man who made it all possible. The man who helped me through the good times as well as the bad. My own personal Jesus, walking with me hand in hand, leading me straight to the light. Leading me to where I needed to be all along.

I tell all the staff, even Jeffrey, goodbye. I thank them for all their hard work and dedication to not only myself, but others like me who have suffered from various mental health diseases. I am given all the belongings I turned in on the first day. I even have my journal handed back to me. I look at it for a few moments before handing it back, telling Jeffrey and McIntosh that I don't need it anymore.

They applaud me and praise me even more as I make my way outside, where I find Maxwell with the limo waiting. I ride alone, as there is no Abel. I am alone, and for the first time in a long time, that feels remarkable. Alone in my head, and I feel free. I feel clear.

When I get home, I am met by Braelynn. She leads me inside, where Sophie tackles my side, hugging me like she never wants to let go. I see friends and family. We celebrate over dinner before I help Braelynn clean the house. I read a story to Sophie before she goes to sleep. I meet Braelynn downstairs. Our lips meet just as our bodies do, embracing like we are falling in love all over again, going through the kitchen and into the living room, onto the couch then the floor, before we reach our final destination.

In the bedroom, we make up for lost time until the sun slowly comes up as sleep consumes us, but only briefly. We wake up and pick up where we left off.

I stand on the back porch, drinking coffee, staring out into the city across from my home, a smile on my face. Life is perfect. I have a beautiful wife and an amazing daughter. I don't mind the dark clouds hanging above, or the faint rain grazing over, the tiny raindrops dripping slowly off my ears, chin, and nose. I chuckle to myself, standing here, soaking it all in. I recall the morning session between Braelynn and I, making love for two hours. I chuckle again, remembering when I told her I needed some coffee after the workout she put me through. I told her that I'd head out to get some stuff to make for breakfast as well.

Sophie has always liked that. Breakfast in bed seems to be her favorite meal of the day. I finish my coffee then head to the fridge, checking to see what was needed for breakfast. Eggs, bacon, milk. The key ingredients were a must. I yell down the hallway to Braelynn, letting her know that I was heading out before my shoes meet the sidewalk, leading me to a local grocery.

I can't deny how great I feel. It's like walking on sunshine, as the song says.

At the store, I grab what I need and make my purchase before heading towards home again. On the way there, something catches my eye off in the distance. Smoke. Black and gray smoke. Coming from the direction of my home.

As I get closer, I can hear them. Braelynn and Sophie. Their agonizing screams, that nearly busted my eardrum. I drop the groceries as I begin to race toward home, but the harder I try to run, the less distance I cover. My legs feel heavy, like I have concrete blocks around my feet. They drag, but I keep pushing forward.

After what feels like an eternity, I finally reach the driveway, but to my horror, everything is burning. I blink once. I see the flames. I blink again, and the smoke swallows me whole. Through the smoke, from what I can see, everything looks dead.

Like everything is gone.

I want to cry, but I can't. I go forward slowly towards the house, kicking rubble to the side. I reach the back porch and it looks fine. Just the way I left it. I open the door, looking inside, to find that everything looks normal. I step back outside, and I can see the flames. I close my eyes, trying to catch my breath, trying to make sense of what I'm seeing, but I can't.

I step back inside, entering the living room where I planned to watch cartoons or whatever Sophie wants to watch. I sit on the couch, still untouched by the flames, and stare at the TV. I run my hands over my face, over my head, closing my eyes in the process.

When I open them, the TV is on. There's a fight scene on display. I can't tell who it is, so I lean forward, only to gasp for air when I see who's fighting. It's two men.

They look familiar.

They are me.

I'm fighting myself.

I can see the lead pipe in my hand, as I hit the other me repeatedly, blood spraying over my face.

And then, I hear a voice. A little girl's voice, to be exact. I turn to see Sophie, sitting next to me, her beautiful face now black and scabbed over. The smell of burnt flesh stings my nostrils. I stare at Sophie as what's left of her speaks, her words sending a chill down my spine as she asks, "Why are you beating yourself up, daddy?"

I fall off the couch as the front door blows off its hinges. A gust of wind travels through our home, attacking Sophie, sweeping her away as she becomes nothing but ashes. I gasp for breath, trying to understand what just happened, trying to figure it out in my mind, but I can't find an answer.

"You left us!"

I turn around and I can't believe my eyes. I see my wife, covered in black and gray, resembling the smoke from earlier. Her flesh burned to a crisp. She's no longer beautiful. She doesn't look anything like the Braelynn I know. There appeared to be nothing left of the woman I made love to earlier this morning. I can tell it's her only from her voice. She speaks again, "You left us!"

"No! No! I went to the grocery store. Nothing more," I cry.

She slowly makes her way down the stairs, each step turning black as her foot touches down. "No, James! You left us and you never came back...."

I stand up, walking towards her, trying to find her beauty somewhere beneath the burnt flesh and discoloration. "I would never leave you, Braelynn. I love you. You are it for me. You should know that. I am not complete without you. I am not complete without Sophie. I can't live without you two. You keep me going. You keep me sane. You give me a reason to live. You know that! You know that, right?! You should know that, Brae. I need you in my life. I need you. I've always needed you and I will always need you. You are my life...."

"You need me?" she says, flesh falls off her cheek, revealing deteriorating muscle and bone. "If you need me, then you would have never left. You would not have left Sophie and me alone. But you did, because you're a selfish bastard. You only think of yourself. That is why you always allow yourself to become a victim."

I shake my head. "No, no, no..."

"You're pathetic," she says before turning and opening the front door. The wind howls as debris flies like a tornado has hit. Braelynn stands in the doorway as she turns. We make eye contact as I watch the wind picks her up, turning her into ash, just as it did with Sophie.

I race toward her, running outside, grabbing any ashes that I can, but to no avail.

I go back inside as the flames finally enter the house, burning everything. The drywall snaps. The glass frames burst as the fire consumes the photos once strung across the wall.

I open the door to Sophie's room, watching as the flames eat her pink comforter, the metal of the bedframe bending due to the heat. It melts her toys, all the memories I have of her burning away into nothing.

I walk into the room I once shared with my wife. The scene is the same as the rest of what used to be our normal home. I lie on the bed as chips fall from the surrounding ceiling. The fire rips through the door, engulfing all we ever shared or owned.

The floor gives way, and I fall. I look up, just waiting for it all to end. I don't feel perfect. I'm no longer walking on sunshine.

I feel nothing.

Until I wake up. My head spins and cracks simultaneously. It takes a few moments for me to regain my bearings. When I do, I realize where I am. I'm in the white room where I was assaulted, once again.

37

The door opens and Jeffrey enters, along with a few other orderlies. They grab me, lifting me off the warm, sticky floor. As they drag me out of the room, I catch a glimpse of my broken and bloodied reflection.

They take me back to my cell in X6, dropping me like a sack of potatoes on my bed. I groan as I roll over. Based on my reflection, I was assaulted again. I have no memory of it.

"You must not have done so well, James."

I look over, staring through the rusty bars to find William peering down at me. I reply, my voice raspy and weak, "How can you tell?"

"It's all over your face," he says with a snicker.

I can't help but laugh through the pain. The hallucination replays through my head. I get to see my wife and daughter burning again before the wind rips them away. I want to scream. I want to cry. I want to do something, but I can't. I hurt too much.

"What's the last thing you remember?" he asks.

"I was in McIntosh's office. I told him I'd do whatever I had to in order to get out of here," I reply in between dry heaves.

"Did he offer you a pill?" William inquires. I nod and he asks, "What color was it?"

I taste blood on the tip of my tongue as I say, "Green."

"And they brought you back here."

"Looks that way," I say, pushing myself up. Sitting up straight, I shrug my shoulders. The bones and muscle ache. "Why are you asking me all this?"

William twiddles his thumbs, his attention focused on that until I ask my question. He looks at me sideways. "That's what they did to me. I just didn't look like you when all was said and done."

"What are you talking about?"

He grabs the bars, appearing to squeeze them as tightly as he can. "It's a test, James. It's all a test. If you want out, you have to pass. And if he's given you the green pill, then you're near the end. If you don't pass the test, then you don't get out of here."

"I don't remember anything about a test. What test?!"

His grip loosens as he slides back slightly, keeping his eyes locked with mine. "You've already failed once. I can tell just by the way you look. You'll only have one more chance. After that, you're here forever."

William scurries away into the darkness of his cell, leaving me alone in my head. Unlike my hallucination, I am not free. I am not clear. I'm anything but. William's words repeat in my mind as I lay back down.

After that, you're here forever.

After that, you're here forever.

You're here forever.

Forever.

38

"I don't know how to get us out of here," Abel says as he paces my cell. My face is slowly healing up, but I haven't forgotten William's mention of a test.

"I've told you that I know what I have to do. I have to give in, Abel. It's as simple as that," I reply, feeling a hint of pain echo through my cheek as my jaw moves.

Abel stops and turns to me. "You say that, but according to your face, it's not as simple as you make it out to be. You couldn't pass the test," he states, using his fingers to make air quotes.

I had told Abel about the test once I finally woke up from a long sleep. He had told me he had taken control, slipping into the driver's seat right before the beating started. He told me that was why I couldn't remember anything.

"Technically, you couldn't pass the test," I reply, "but I guess it's all the same."

Abel looks down, slowly nodding. "I know I couldn't. I knew what McIntosh wanted me to do. What he wanted you to do. I knew if you and I...if we crossed that line...it would be you who suffered for it. I knew you wouldn't be able to live with the guilt."

"Abel," I say, "look at me." He shakes his head and I tell him to look at me once again. He still shakes his head. I finally shout, "Look! At! Me!" This startles other patients around, all of them looking up and down at me, depending on their position in X6. I don't care, though. I'm pissed off. My own mind working against me. I didn't come to Trinity for any of this to happen. I came here for a cure, but the only cure this place has to offer is violence.

Abel finally looks at me. "What?"

I exhale, realizing I haven't asked a certain question of Abel after he told me he took the brunt of the abuse. "What did McIntosh want me to do?"

"You don't want to know, James. You truly don't," he states, shaking his head as his back rests against the cell bars.

"Yes, I do. I need to know. More than you could ever possibly imagine."

"You forget," Abel says, pushing off the bars, "we share the same brain." He points to the side of his head. "I can imagine the same things you do."

I scoff. "Yet, we have continuously kept one another in the dark on so much."

"Exactly," he says, clapping his hands together. "So, what's one more thing?"

"You don't get to decide that!" I shout, stumbling up from my bed where I've stayed since I was dragged back here. My outburst causes some patients to shout expletives in my direction. Some even grab the bars and shake them like angry gorillas at the zoo. We are all kings of the jungle in X6. All of us ready to bust out and run rampant it seems.

"I have to make some decisions without your consent, James. I'm sorry," Abel exclaims. He points at a bruise on my face. "I chose to take that beating."

"Because you were born to protect me," I say, rolling my eyes. "I've heard that one too many times, Abel. I don't need you to protect me anymore. Now, answer my question!" I demand, stepping closer toward him.

"No," he says.

I grab Abel, shoving him into the bars. Part of me knows I'm not physically grabbing him, but it feels real to me all the same. We lock eyes as I scream, "TELL ME!" The patients, the inmates, the wild animals cheer me on, feeding off my display of aggression like the good puppets McIntosh has turned them into.

"Alright, alright," Abel says, letting out a sigh. "He wanted you to cross the line."

"What line?" I ask, taking a step back.

He continues, "He brought you to that room. Locking you in there with the same guys he had beat the shit out of you before. He wanted you to fight back. He wanted you to go further. He gave you that pill, thinking it would drive you to hurt them. Badly."

He continues, but I drown him out, knowing what he means. I know what the good doctor wants me to do. It's become clearer. A display of violence isn't going to be enough. He wants more. Much more. And Abel is right, it's a line that I won't cross.

But then, I think about my freedom.

"I need to be tested again," I say, locking eyes with Abel.

He shakes his head again. "No. No, James. You can't. You're not doing this to yourself. And after being here, I don't think I am, either."

"This isn't about you, Abel. I've told you that from the start. I have to do this. I want out of here," I say, "and I will get out of here. By any means necessary."

"Now," he scoffs, "I know what everyone has meant when they've told you that you're letting them win. This will be their victory lap, James. They don't deserve a damn thing."

I shake my head, letting out a deep breath of crippling defeat. "I know, Abel. I know. I'm not going to argue with you anymore. I'm not going to argue with them, either. This is McIntosh's world," I say, lifting my hands up as I stretch my arms out, as if I am putting X6 on display for the entire world. "I'm living in it. I have to give him what he wants if I want to escape these walls."

Abel sighs now, shaking his head. "I know you want out. I want you out of here as well, so let me do it. Let me give that bastard what he wants. Your hands don't have to be dirty. I was born so mine could be. So I could take the hit for you."

I shake my head once again. "No, not this time, Abel. This is something I need to do on my own. You can't take over. You can't be anywhere near me when this happens."

"You know I can't do that, James."

His words echo in my ears as I stand, facing the bars. I take a deep breath, holding it for a few moments as I think of all I've lost, and all I could regain upon leaving here before I exhale, turning to Abel as I reply, "You know I have to do this, Abel."

He says nothing as I stare at him. I blink, and he's gone. I tell myself it must be this way. It is what McIntosh has wanted all along. Time to give the devil his due, I tell myself before I tap my knuckles against the bars.

39

I think about one of my sessions with McIntosh and how he compared me to a fighter. I envision myself stepping into the ring and how I'd unleash any and all pent-up frustration. I'd think about my thrilling victories as well as my heartbreaking losses as I am led by an entourage of orderlies out of X6. I think about the feel of the ring, warm from the fight taking place. I can smell the sweat, not only of myself, but an opponent for a moment or two, before we step outside.

I remember that want, that need, to fight back against bullies in school, and how I didn't want to rely on Abel. I joined the wrestling team, learning grapples as well as building strength and endurance. I'd lift weights daily, putting my body through the grind, hitting lift after lift until my muscles broke down through exhaustion. I built muscle and I was able to slam an attacker with ease, but it wasn't enough.

I got a part-time job, and I joined a gym. I learned to box, and my trainer loved my aggression. I picture him for a minute, asking myself if it was McIntosh in disguise, as they shared an affinity for the violence coursing through my veins.

That violence came in handy the older I got. I didn't always need Abel, I remind myself. I remember fighting Dewayne and his buddies after school a few times. It would always be three on one, but I handled myself well, walking away with a few scrapes and bruises, leaving them a little worse for wear.

That violence was supposed to serve me well when I went pro, fighting my way to the top of the sport. That was when Abel was alive and well. Not to mention at his worst. I think about how he was a stalker. A woman beater. All the things I was not, because I kept him suppressed for far too long. I felt he sought vengeance against me.

So, I became a social worker, burying him by helping others. Or trying at least.

I remind myself that I came here to Trinity to get rid of him, fearful of the harm he could cause, just as he had done years prior.

I wanted to get rid of him.

And now, I feel I need him more than ever.

I know if I let Abel in, he would be able to take the fight to the orderlies. That he could maim them before making a break for the front door. I know he could probably make it out alive.

I know I can't, therefore I do nothing.

I follow the leader, the leader, the leader.

My mind shifts. I see me standing across the ring from an opponent. He's not facing me. I stand in my black trunks, banging my fists together, ready to fight with all I have, when he turns around, removing the hood of his leather white robe, with its blood-red trim.

His identity is revealed as I find myself staring into the eyes of McIntosh. His stare is as devilish as the smirk of his lips.

I can hear the bell ring and I see me rushing towards him, throwing not only caution to the wind, but my fists as hard and as fast as I can.

But every punch misses his face. McIntosh laughs at me as he dodges my attack. I swing wide and jab straight, yet he deflects each attempt. And then, he lands a shot to my jaw. It staggers me, hitting me like a ton of bricks.

I swing again, and he blocks it once more before hitting me with an uppercut, knocking me down to the mat.

When I hit the mat, I return to reality, finding myself outside the room. The orderlies stand in straight lines, one on each side of me, with Jeffrey standing at the center of the door. His hands cupped together, a smile on his face, as always, he looks at me.

"Are you ready, James?"

Abel screams echo in my head. Our head. He tells me not to do this. I take a deep breath, focusing all my attention to Jeffrey, until Abel's voice is no more. I wait until it is dead silent on all fronts in my head before I say, "Yes."

Hands and arms grab me out of nowhere, wrestling me into position before something sharp stabs into my right forearm. I glance down as the needle enters the vein. A burning sensation follows.

At first, I see flashes of my life away from Trinity. I see me spending time with Braelynn, walking through Central Park, having a picnic with the sun shining on us. I see me running through the grass, chasing Sophie as she glances over her shoulder at me mid-pursuit, all smiles and giggles.

But then what I see becomes something else. The happiness is replaced with anger. I see flashes of violence. My fights in the ring, hurting my opponents. And then, I see sins I have yet to commit. Flashes of violence against people I've never met.

I see me running through the streets of New York, terrorizing and attacking anyone and everyone within range. I see my hands grabbing individuals, slamming them to the ground before beating them until my skin is covered in their blood. I see my teeth grinding on flesh, the metallic taste of their blood warming my tongue.

And then, I see Jeffrey opening the door before I'm shoved inside the room. Lights come on.

In between flashes of violence, the room comes into view. I turn to my left, and I see McIntosh standing behind double-paned glass, his arms folded across his chest, his eyes staring at me. He reaches down, pressing a button as his voice echoes in the room, "Are you ready, James?"

I nod.

He says, "This will be your last shot. I don't want you to be a failure, James, but if you are, then…" he sighs, "Then, you will spend the rest of your days here."

I feel my shoulders moving up and down at a rapid pace, adrenaline running rampant. "If I give you what you want…" I see me busting through the glass somehow, grabbing him by the throat, sinking my teeth in like a rabid animal, "will you let me leave?"

"You can leave as soon as it's done, if you wish."

I nod. "I'll do whatever I have to," I say, the violence swelling up in my muscles, my mind focusing on my anger, when the door opens again. The anger and violence begin to deteriorate when Lance is shoved into the room, looking helpless and confused, like a mouse being fed to a snake.

I hear McIntosh say, "We will put that to the test."

40

It is years ago and David McIntosh rests in his room, on his perfectly made bed, a textbook in his hands. His eyes study the words, trying to make sense of the medical terminology. A small smirk forms from his lips as he daydreams of being a doctor.

He doesn't want to be just a regular doctor. He doesn't want to go on to be one of those doctors that children come to see before getting a lollipop or balloon after each visit. McIntosh, as his friends call him, wants to be a brain surgeon.

His grandfather passed away from dementia. McIntosh wasn't sure what it was at first, but after extensive reading, he knows the power it has on the mind. Researching the mind couldn't be called a fascination, as that would be an understatement. He knows some may call it an obsession, but that is fine by him.

His eyes continue to scan the words, his brain processing the knowledge he sees, retaining it. His friends call him a nerd, and those friends have dwindled down over the years, ever since he decided to pick up a book, to learn. His brain has truly become a sponge, soaking the knowledge in, expanding from his constant learning.

But for all he learns, McIntosh knows there will always be people who disapprove. He knows there will be plenty of people in his life who do not care for knowledge. People like his friends.

Like his father.

His father wants him to grow up to be just like him. He expects McIntosh to become a plumber or an electrician. To do a real man's work. The son knows his father couldn't care less for him, therefore he couldn't care less about what his father wants.

******

David McIntosh graduates at the top of his class. He makes his way into the top program in the United States. He excels, despite not caring all that much for a social life. The friends he makes do not compare to his thirst for knowledge.

It doesn't take him long however, to realize just how alone and bored he is. McIntosh decides to head out into the big city near the university. What he finds is a whole other world. A world he has never truly seen or allowed himself to see. He feels alien as he enters the bars.

This soon becomes his life. He knows his father would be proud. He always wanted his son to become one of the guys. He was always pushy, until McIntosh's father received a push that sent him tumbling down the stairs to the basement, cracking his neck along the way. The son remembers breathing a sigh of relief, knowing he would never need to try to meet the father's expectations again.

He wants to reach his own. He downs a few drinks then strikes up a conversation with a pretty girl. She seems to enjoy his vocabulary, but then again, he tells himself, it could be the alcohol. She will do just fine, McIntosh thinks, offering to buy her another drink, which she accepts.

Using precise speed, McIntosh slips the crushed pill into her drink. He watches intensely as she downs the liquid in one shot. He knows how the brain works. It won't take long for things to spin like a top.

He takes her back to his room. They talk until she falls asleep. What he does next, she will not remember, but McIntosh will enjoy for as long as he can.

The next morning, this girl wakes up. Her name is Judith, but she goes by Judy. She states her head is hurting. She asks him if anything happened last night. He tells her no. She looks down and sees her clothes are still on. Judy calls him a real gentleman. All he can do is smile while thinking of how gentle and precise he was when placing the clothes back on after cleaning the mess, getting rid of any residual evidence.

******

He stands at the test subject after peeling the skin back, exposing the brain. He studies it for a few moments, trying to remember what he must do. His hands move, the scalpel clutched between his fingers, but the precision isn't there. The hands shake like a leaf on a tree when hit by a slight breeze.

He fails his test. He blames Judy. He punishes her just as his father did his mother when he was a child. It is the only thing he ever kept from his father. That scolding temperament. He knows Judy should leave, just as he knows that she won't. She apologizes to him for keeping him up the night before his big test. She accepts full blame, telling McIntosh that she loves him.

******

David McIntosh sits at the bar. It is the cheapest place for him to drink his sorrows away. He feels sorrow for feeling sorry. He recalls never being depressed when his father died. Sure, it was by his hand, but still. He felt no real sadness as the years went on.

No real guilt. Not even for his past sins with his girlfriend, Judy. What makes him sad is the fact that he is without a true job. He is without a true career path. His hopes and dreams of becoming a brain surgeon have all but died. Judy is pregnant with their child, to top it off.

McIntosh drinks to that. He can care less about Judy, but he wants his child to have a future. He wants to be able to provide, but right now he can't. Seeing the man in the flashy suit next to him makes McIntosh sick to his stomach.

Then the suit says, "You look like a man down on his luck."

He takes a swig of his drink before giving the suit his full attention, "What gave that away?"

"I've watched you guzzle Jim Beam down for the last hour. The way it looks to me right now is that there is no stopping you, David McIntosh."

"Do I know you?"

The suit shakes his head.

"Then how do you know my name?" McIntosh asks, feeling his frustration slowly turn to something else. Something he has never really felt before.

Fear.

"I know all about you," the suit says in a soft but haunting voice. McIntosh can see the skin of the man's face. It is worn, and his eyes tell the story of someone who has seen some shit and survived.

"What...what do you know?" the would-be doctor asks, cursing himself for allowing his voice to break.

"I know you wanted to be a brain surgeon. I know you've missed out on a lot of life in order to do so. I also know you graduated at the top of your class before flunking your big test. You couldn't quite keep it together, could you, David?"

"What is this? What do you want?"

"I want to offer you a job, so calm the hell down."

His voice cracks again as McIntosh asks, "A job... a job?" He shakes his head, trying to regain a sense of calm. The calm he had during his studies. The calm he had when he had his way with Judy, before she fell in love. Taking a deep breath, the calm slowly arrives, and he looks the suit in the eyes. "What sort of job?"

A smirk appears. "Government job."

The calm remains, slowly beginning to blend in with a rising excitement. "Doing what?"

"We can talk business soon. Right now, we can drink. Just know that whatever I tell you will change your life. It will be an offer you can't refuse. And if you try to," the suit says, turning away and staring at his reflection in the mirror behind the shelves housing the top-brand alcohol, "just know I've killed people. Many people. It's my job. I have no qualms doing it again. I'd hate for your child to grow up without a father."

Working with the government will help, McIntosh tells himself as he ignores the chill racing up and down his spine. I can provide a future for myself, as well as my child.

They both order drinks and finish them just as quickly. Wiping any residue from his mustache, McIntosh says, "When you're ready to talk, I'm all ears."

41

"You know something, James?" I watch as McIntosh begins pacing slowly back and forth in the opposite room. "When I was first offered this job...no, no," he says, shaking his head, "this opportunity... yes, because that is what this is. It's an opportunity. When it was offered to me, I was told there is a dark fever plaguing our great nation."

Keeping my eyes on him, I ask, "What the hell are you rambling on about?"

He scoffs, "I'll tell you. This dark fever is something the media likes to play off of. They use it to get ratings. You see all the random shootings in the name of religion or whatever one's heart desires. That is due to this dark fever. I was told America lives for violence. It was built off violence. Look at what happened when settlers came overseas. It was complete genocide and what do we give Native Americans to make up for the misfortune we bestowed upon them?" he shrugs. "The answer to that is laughable."

"Let's not forget slavery. That led to a difference of opinion, which led to civil war, brother against brother. Everyone who participated in that genocide, in that war, or any war afterwards...they all suffered from that dark fever," he continues.

I stand in the center of the room, watching as he continues to pace, his words resonating slightly. "As human beings, we are brought up to be violent. It is in our DNA. We have no way of truly stopping it. Someone may seem quiet and meek, but sooner or later..." he cackles, "sooner or later, that violent side will show its face. It's just who we are as individuals. We create war, famine, so on and so forth. We live, we breathe, we kill anyone and everything around us in some fashion."

I finally cut him off, "What does that have to do with me?"

"I believe," he stops in the center of the other room, lining himself up with me, "We've only seen the tip of the iceberg with you. You, James, are my favorite subject. I don't want that to be ruined. That is why I need you to give in and let that side of yourself out."

I roll my eyes. "And how the hell do I do that?"

Then, the door opens. I look away from McIntosh, watching as one of the orderlies tosses something to the ground.

"This is how," I hear McIntosh say.

My eyes dart from Lance to McIntosh in a repetitive motion. "What the hell do you mean?"

"Only one of you will leave this room on your own. The other person won't be as lucky."

I shake my head. "No, I'm not doing this," I say, understanding now what Abel was trying to keep me from.

"James, you have no other choice," McIntosh says, pulling up a chair and taking a seat behind the glass, like a moviegoer in a theater, anxiously waiting for some superhero summer blockbuster to begin.

Before I have a chance to speak, Lance charges at me, driving the top of his head into my chest. I grab him and try to wrestle him down, but I can't. He drives a fist into my ribs, causing me to loosen my grip. His other fist connects with my jaw, staggering me.

I try to catch my breath, but Lance doesn't give me a chance. He wraps both hands around my neck before driving his knees into my ribs and chest.

"Oh, James. This is just disappointing," McIntosh states.

I struggle to break free of Lance, but he positions himself behind me, wrapping his right bicep over my throat. I grab at his arm as he begins to squeeze. I recall how innocent Lance seemed when we first met. How he told me to keep my head up. I think about how I don't want to hurt him.

But then, I catch glimpses of my wife and child. Seeing them reminds me of how badly I want to go home.

Lance continues to squeeze, and I stop fighting. I know the more I struggle, the tighter his grip will become. I work to slow myself, to slip into a slight calm.

"Where's that fight, James? I thought you wanted out of here?" McIntosh shouts into the intercom like a menacing spectator watching Lance try to kill me for his mere amusement.

I think of my family once more before switching into another gear. I'm still in the driver's seat as I manage to pry Lance's arm from around my throat before driving my elbow over and over into his ribs. His guttural screams echo in the room, before we both scramble to our feet. I lunge forward, connecting with a shot to his jaw, dropping Lance back to the floor as I get to my feet, catching my breath.

"What are you waiting for, James?" McIntosh chimes in. "If you want to see your family again, let that violent side out. Let it run wild. Let it be free."

Abel tells me he will take care of things. That I need to let him in. I shake my head and slam my fists into my face repeatedly, as if I'm beating Abel out of my head as I tell him no over and over. I stop as I see Lance climb to his feet. He spits out blood before charging at me.

I see Braelynn. Her smile. I smell her scent. It reminds me of home.

Lance gets closer.

I see Sophie. Her smile warms me for a split second. Her voice echoes in my ears.

He gets closer.

I tell myself what I must do to see them again. I grab Lance by the back of the head and drive his skull into the wall. He stumbles back and I tackle him to the floor. I think of my fights and the different strategies I've used. How violent I've allowed myself to become in order to survive and win.

Lance out-wrestles me, sitting on my chest. He lands punch after punch. Pain echoes in my body as I try to fight back, but I'm unable to move. He strikes me again and again.

I taste blood. I feel it run down the side of my face. I tell myself I'm not getting out of here.

I repeat Abel's words to me from that day in school. Get up. Fight back. Get up. Fight back.

Lance goes to strike, but I catch his arm before pulling closer. I lock him in a chokehold and I whisper, "We don't have to do this. Just stop. Please. Just stop." He struggles. "Damn it, Lance. Please stop!"

Lance connects with another blow to my ribs. I lose my grip, but I roll over, grabbing anything that I can to keep him down on the ground. I climb on top, driving my knees into his chest and throat.

I look down at him, and I don't see Lance.

I see Dewayne, and I strike.

I see my father. My mother. I see Quentin, remembering how I failed him. I strike over and over.

I picture everything that I have hated in the world. The people. The situations. Everything that makes it unsafe for my child to walk around. Everything that has caused me to end up places like Trinity.

And I strike. I strike until there is nothing left. I strike until realization hits me like a punch to the gut, knocking the wind out of me. I look down at Lance and I see his bloody, battered face. He gasps for air and I just gasp as I push myself away from him.

I crawl toward him, hearing the door open behind me. Something hits the ground near us, but I keep my eyes on Lance. I tell him I'm sorry. I apologize over and over, until I catch a glimpse of his fingers wrapped around a lead pipe,

It was the something that hit the ground, and Lance is bringing it full force toward my skull. I block it then grapple it from him. I lift it high above my head. I glare at him. I don't see Lance anymore.

I see Abel. I see myself. I see McIntosh.

I bring the pipe down.

And, I'm sorry.

I'm sorry.

I'm sorry.

I'm...

42

My body aches and throbs as I am led back to my room. I'm no longer in X6. No concrete tomb in solitary. I'm back in my very first room at Trinity. It is still dark outside. I know this because Jeffrey and his gang of orderlies dragged me through the damp night grass.

I rest on my bed. It feels foreign, like I've never been here before, but I feel like I can finally rest in peace.

Yet, I don't.

I can't sleep.

All I can do is replay all the things I've done. I still feel the pipe in my hand. My muscles remain jarred. I see it over and over again.

Lance's face. Or what is left of it. I can hear his screams. I feel his skin tear against the bone of my knuckles. I see the pipe coming down. Then, there's blood spraying across my face. Across the floor.

Then, I see his teeth as they skid towards the wall.

McIntosh's voice echoes in my head, "Do it, James! Do it! Hit him! Hit him again! He wants to kill you! He wants to keep you from your family! You can't let him do that, James!"

I see Lance's face again.

McIntosh screams at me, "Hit him! Hit him again!"

I'm sorry. I'm sorry. I'm sorry.

I'm sorry. I'm...

I beg God or whoever to just let me sleep. To let me have a semblance of peace in this seemingly never-ending nightmare.

But sleep doesn't come. The nightmare continues. God makes no appearance.

I relive my crime like the guilty party I am.

"James?"

Abel's voice fills the room. I roll over and face him. "What?"

He looks at me, only to lower his gaze and shake his head.

"Did you come here to say 'I told you so?' If that's why you're here then just leave. I don't need it. I don't want it," I say, the words seething through my teeth, connected to my pain-filled gums.

"I don't think I need to say that. It doesn't matter now."

"Why?" I ask.

"You've crossed a line."

"It's a line you wanted me to cross before. Why is it such a bad thing now?" I hiss.

Abel paces back and forth, his arms over his chest. "I've seen what you've become, James. At least who you were before you came here. You had worked very hard to be a decent person. You worked hard to erase the damage I had caused. I didn't want you to ever go back there. That is why I was willing to get my hands dirty. I wanted you to keep yours clean."

I look at my hands. They are far from clean.

"Abel," I say.

He stops pacing and we lock eyes. "Yes?"

I think about Braelynn. Memories of spending time with her and my daughter flash in my head. I want to cry, but I can't. I exhale, feeling the tears build but never fall. "I don't want to be here anymore."

He nods. "I know, but you did what he wanted. You're going home."

I shake my head. "No. That's not what I meant. I don't want to be here anymore."

"What are you talking about?" he asks. I can tell by the look in his eyes that he knows exactly what I mean. He just doesn't want to admit it.

Neither do I.

I sigh, "We both know that you know what I mean."

He lies, "No I don't."

"I know you do."

148

43

"You deserve this, James…" I say as I look through my cell phone, seeing the pictures of Braelynn and Sophie. Seeing their smiles makes me smile before I mutter to myself, "You deserve this, James…"

The phone rings yet again. It is Braelynn. I realize it's been nearly an hour since I spoke with her last. I answer it. "Hello?"

"Hey, babe…" Braelynn sighs, "I called you almost an hour ago. Where are you? When are you coming home?"

I look around the apartment, not sure if it is safe for me to exit the room. I look down then close my eyes, letting out a deep breath, telling myself that I am going to have to get it over with at some point. That I have to go to that house.

"James?"

Hearing her say my name feels unnatural. I take a deep breath then exhale just as hard. "Yeah."

"When are you coming home? Is everything okay?"

Gripping the phone in my hand, pressing it hard against the side of this skull of mine, "Everything's fine."

"Well, when are you coming home?"

I sigh, "I'm coming…I'm coming home."

She sighs as well. "Well, please come home. I'm ready for you to be home, as is Sophie."

"I'll be there."

"Be safe. I love you," she says.

Hearing those words sends a shockwave through my body. I take another deep breath, exhaling as I pull the phone away. I bring it back and I say, "I love you," trying to make it sound as meaningful as possible. "I'll see you soon," I say weakly before ending the call.

I take another look at the pictures, my eyes resting on a specific one where Braelynn is hugging Sophie, and I say, "I can't fail again."

I leave the apartment, getting into my vehicle. At first, it doesn't feel like mine. I sit in it for a few moments, replaying memories in my head of when it was first purchased, and various trips it had been used for, before starting it up and driving through the city. Everything feels and looks otherworldly due to where I have been in the last month and a half.

Once I arrive home, I stop a block or so down from it. I sit in my vehicle, just staring at it. I question myself, asking if I should get out and go inside. What happens when I get in there? Am I going to be expected to show love and compassion? How do I even do that? I ask myself these things over and over again before I realize I've been sitting in my vehicle for fifteen minutes.

I get out and walk the block or so until I am at the bottom of the steps leading to the front deck. I tell myself that I have to do this. Each step I take feels heavier than the first, and before I know it, I'm at the front door. I take another deep breath, hating the fact I've been filled with such fear since getting out of Trinity.

I go to knock on the door before remembering I have keys. I test a few before finding the right key. I open the door ever so gently, feeling the quiet and not liking it at all. I close the door behind me, when lights flip on.

"SURPRISE!!!"

Voices echo through the house, startling me. I see Braelynn. I see Kerri as well, which to me is incredibly awkward, given what happened between us the last time we spoke. I see Sophie standing with Eliza and her new lover. Sophie rushes over to me, hugging me at the waist. I actually smile at this before lifting her up in arms and hugging her as tightly as I can, as I feel he would do.

Braelynn walks over. She hugs me and stands up on her tippy toes to kiss me. I kiss her back, and it feels as real as anything else I've ever felt. She hugs me then whispers into my ear, "Now you see why I was frantically calling you."

I whisper back, "I had a feeling you had something planned. I'm not much for surprises."

She steps back, looking at me slightly confused as a smirk appears on her face, "Don't give me that crap. You know I'm your wife, right? I know a lot about you. I know you're all about surprises. You remember when you proposed? That was clever as shit, babe. I know better."

I crack a grin. "Of course, I remember." I look at Sophie. "You remember too, don't you?" I ask, trying to hide the fact that I am struggling to put it all together.

Sophie nods. "Of course, dad! You proposed to her in the comic book shop."

I laugh. "Well, duh! Who could forget something like that?"

"Brae, I want some food," Sophie says as I let her down. Brae smiles before taking Sophie's hand, leading her into the kitchen. I step further into the living room area. I give the other guests a wave and a nod.

I walk over to Eliza and her boyfriend. "Hey, guys. One of you could have told me my wife was throwing a surprise party for me."

Eliza interjects, "Let's not worry with all that." The boyfriend nods before heading off in the other direction. "Anyway," Eliza continues, "How are you feeling?"

I grin. "Like I've been to Hell and back. I feel like this is going to take some getting used to, but I believe I'll manage."

Eliza nods. "I can understand that, but just remember, that little girl over there," she says, pointing into the kitchen where I see Brae and Sophie, all smiles and laughing, "loves you with all of her being. Sometimes I feel she loves you more than she does me, and while that is a bummer, I still have to protect her. You can't do this to her again, James. She asked me every single day to call you or Brae to see if you were okay."

I look down, stuffing my hands in my pockets. "I didn't know how it'd affect her. All I can say is that I'm sorry."

"You don't have to make it up to me, James…" Eliza says, "you have to make it up to her, and you better do so."

"I will," I say with a nod before walking away, keeping my eyes focused on Braelynn and Sophie. I walk a little further, only for another face to stop me. "Kerri," I say with a grin. Kerri, the woman who caused a chain reaction a few years ago, smiles at me.

"Hello, James. Welcome home."

Kerri worked in connection with my old agency, providing shelter to victims of domestic violence, as well as runaway children.

She and I were great friends, at some point. This was before Braelynn came into the picture, and I wanted more. She didn't seem interested, from what I remember, but hope was always held for some reason.

After the attack on Darren, she had asked me to lunch. It seemed like a good idea, but then I remembered she had been nice to me, maybe even a little flirty at times, and I quickly forgot about Braelynn.

The memory plays in my head.

I see us sitting outside of a brewery, at a picnic table, both of us drinking beer. She struggles with her hair as it keeps falling in her face due to the consistent breeze rushing over us.

"I'm going to get a haircut. I can't stand this mess," she says, with a slight giggle.

"No, don't do that," I reply, giving a tiny grin. "It's one of your best features."

She shoots me a look, telling me my statement was a little awkward. She grins either way. "Thanks, I guess." I watch as she takes a sip of her beer, my eyes watching her neck, revealing itself to be soft, and how I can't get over this urge to wrap my hands around it, to squeeze it even for just a little bit. "So, what happened with you and Darren?"

I grin, as images of me slamming Darren's head into the wall, driving my fist into his face over and over run through my mind. I can't help but feel pleased with myself. Maybe a little too much, but so be it. "He said some shit that he shouldn't have said. And I let him know how I felt about it."

"But you guys are friends, James."

I remember grinding my teeth together and shaking my head. "No, no. He was just a means to an end. He was just stupid."

"Why are you saying that?" I shush her, pressing my index finger to her lips. "What are you doing?" she asks, and I can tell she's like me, getting more than annoyed about this entire situation.

"Only what feels natural. Let's not talk about Darren. Let's talk about us."

"Are you insane? You're fucking married, James."

"The heart wants what it wants. Isn't that how the song goes?"

"I'm getting out of here." Kerri stands up, quickly gathering her things.

I grab her wrist. "You're not going anywhere. I want to talk."

She struggles a bit, before I loosen my grip, allowing her to pull away. "I don't want to, James. I don't know what's gotten into you, but you..." she pauses for a few moments. "You're not you."

"What the hell do you know?" I hiss. "You don't know me. You had the chance to really know me a few years ago, but you blew that. Didn't you?"

By now, people are looking at us. I pay them no mind. She looks to them for help. At least that is what I see out of the corner of my eye.

"I'm leaving."

"Good. You need to. I'd hate to have what happened to Darren happen to you."

She stares at me, frightened. "Excuse me?"

I stare back, but the longer I stare, the further away she becomes. As the memory fades, all I can hear is my voice, except a little softer.

"What's wrong?"

The words echo in my head, before I find myself no longer at the brewery, but in the living room of my home.

"Thank you. I'll be honest. I'm shocked you're here," I say, as I sense a memory releasing from the pockets of my mind. I know it's going to be a bad one, due to the last time she and I saw one another.

"And I'll be honest too..." she pauses as she glances down for a few moments, letting out a deep breath, like she has practiced this and its not going the way she thought it would, "I came here...to see how you were, and because I felt someone from work should be here."

I look around, "I don't think I left the greatest of impressions there," I say, realizing none of my former co-workers are here.

"Can you really blame them?"

I shake my head no. "I can't. What I did to Darren was horrible, and I'm not even sure that's the best word to describe it."

"I don't think you can," she states, looking down again, "And what happened between us," Kerri pauses, brushing her auburn hair out of her eyes, "I'm trying very hard to forgive and forget."

"How's that going?"

She shrugs, "Difficult. I don't know if I can forget, which makes..."

I cut her off, "Which makes it harder to forgive." I nod. "I get it. I understand. Just know that what happened, it won't happen again. I had no control, but I have it now."

"You think so?"

"I hope so. After all, we…" I pause, trying to catch myself, hoping she didn't pick up on my screw-up, "I mean, I… went through before and during treatment, I think it would be best practice to have as much hope so possible."

"What do you mean by what you went through during treatment?"

I shake my head, "I don't want to get into that right now. How's Darren doing? Hell, how is everyone at the agency?"

"Well, you know I work at the shelter, so I only hear things in passing. Darren recovered fairly well from everything," she says, and I can sense the uneasiness in her voice. "The agency is still recovering as best they can after Quentin's death. I guess its safe to say that everyone is still in shock."

I exhale deeply. "I can't say I blame them." Images of the crime scene flash in my mind as the words escape my lips. "As with you, I don't know if I will ever be able to forget what I saw."

She goes to reply, but I cut her off once again. "I'm sorry, Kerri. About everything. It was never my intention to hurt you in any way. I hope things get better for all of us." I swallow. "I really need to be with my wife and daughter. Thank you for coming," I say, extending my hand as a show of good faith.

Kerri nods. "By all means," she says, taking my hand after a few moments of hesitation, shaking it. "I appreciate your words. I hope you mean them, as I meant it when I wished you the best with everything, James."

I say nothing else.

I nod, giving an unsure grin before stepping away, telling myself it would be best to stay away from her, out of fear of a mental relapse.

44

I enter the kitchen, picking Sophie up into my arms once again. I place an arm around Braelynn, pulling her close. I take a look around, telling myself that all of these people care about me. They are here for me, and I tell myself that while I don't deserve this, that I will make the most of it.

The party continues, and it ends. Everyone says their good lucks and their goodbyes before I see them out, thanking them once again for coming. Eliza says Sophie wants to stay with me, so I spend the rest of the night with her, watching a movie before making sure she gets ready for bed. Once she is ready, she asks me to read her a bedtime story. I read until she falls asleep. I kiss her on the forehead, telling myself that is something good fathers do.

I meet Braelynn back downstairs. I help her clean up before she kisses me. I kiss her back, feeling like I am tasting passion for the very first time. I make love to her in the downstairs living room area. It isn't rough as it was with Julia. It feels real and brand new at the same time. We lie next to one another on the floor until she falls asleep. Once she is resting peacefully, I carry her upstairs and tuck her in. I check on Sophie, remembering the night I broke into Eliza's apartment, almost smothering her. I shake my head, telling myself that things aren't going to be like that now. I kiss her on the forehead once again before exiting the room, heading back downstairs.

I step into the downstairs bathroom, flipping on the light, looking at my reflection, seeing myself as I really am. I run my fingers over the scars as I whisper, "I tried to take all of this from you before, James...." I look down for a few moments, shaking my head, telling myself to get it together. "You were always the strongest, James. You never gave yourself enough credit. I didn't give you enough credit…."

I look up, staring into my eyes, "I know you're in there somewhere, James. I don't know how or when, but I will do all that I can to bring you back. This…all those people who care about you, who showed up to show their love and support for you…I don't deserve it. You do…." I nod. "You do, James. Until you come back, I will fight to keep your memory alive." I let out a sigh as I finish speaking. I continue looking at my reflection, contemplating what's next, before telling myself that whatever it is, I just need to ask myself one question.

What would James do?

45

David McIntosh cannot wait to get home. It's the beginning of a ten-day vacation. A much-needed vacation to say the least. Working with the patients has worn him down and he is ready to kick back, relax, and enjoy being with his family. His daughter is going to be home as well, and it is going to be the first time he has seen her in quite some time.

The traffic in New York is hell, especially with the holidays coming up. McIntosh is okay with it, at least for today, as he has planned on not moving from his favorite recliner once his ass touches the seat. He will get to binge watch all his favorite shows that he has missed. Working with his clients became very trying on him despite how much he enjoys his work, making breakthroughs with his research.

Stuck in traffic, McIntosh presses his head against the headrest, closing his eyes for a few moments, drowning out the noise surrounding him, enjoying the serene calm.

Until his phone rings.

It's his wife, Judy. He had just spoken to her thirty minutes before, so he isn't sure why she is calling again.

"Where are you?" At the very sound of her voice, McIntosh can tell something is wrong. His wife was very laid back, meaning it took a lot to upset her. The tone of her voice indicates something far worse than her being upset.

"I'm stuck in traffic but I'm hoping to be home in the next half hour. Is everything alright? You sound distraught."

There is a silence on the other end of the phone. McIntosh starts to feel his serenity slipping at a rapid pace. "Judy...please answer me. Tell me what's wrong."

Finally, she speaks. "The...the...the police are here." Hearing that the police are at his home fills McIntosh with a sense of dread. He fears they have received information about his research, but then Judy speaks again, her words causing the dread to increase. "They...they ...they found her car..."

McIntosh doesn't want to ask, feeling like he already knows the answer, but he feels beyond weak. "Whose car?"

He listens to his wife quietly sobbing, "Stephanie's..."

A million things begin running through McIntosh's mind. All of them negative. All the worst-case scenarios flash through his head. He closes his eyes as he makes a fist, drawing in a deep breath and violently exhaling. "I will be home as soon as I can, Judy. Try to stay calm, okay?" McIntosh knows it is easier said than done, as he could feel his own struggle to remain calm. "Try to think positive...okay... I must go. I love you...Bye...."

The rest of the drive takes all he has. He wants to throw up. He wants to cry and curse God, but he doesn't. He handles himself just as he did his patients, just as he has his wife, repeating over and over to be positive.

******

McIntosh finally reaches home. He lives in what so many consider a 'fancy' house. His years as a psychologist and scientist, learning how the mind worked, have brought him and his family luxury after luxury. For so long they lived like kings, but on tonight, he feels like anything but a king. He feels like a prisoner.

He stops himself in the foyer, his eyes resting on a photograph of his daughter, Stephanie. It's her high school graduation photo. He remembers how proud he was of her. How proud he has remained. Stephanie had wanted to follow in her father's footsteps and McIntosh recalls being apprehensive about it but realized that his daughter would end up being better than he was, and by better, he meant as a human being.

Just like his patients, McIntosh has had a dark side of his own, filled with secrets that not many people knew of.

"Dr. McIntosh?" calls a voice, breaking McIntosh from his trance. He turns to find a young, strapping lad standing before him in a three-piece suit, his hair combed to the right in a neat and tidy manner. He nods as the young lad extends his hand. "I'm Detective Jacob Cruise. Pleasure to meet you, but I am sorry it is under these circumstances."

He takes the detective's hand before running his free hand over his own head and face as he nods once more. "Yeah, thank you for being here. Speaking of being here," McIntosh says, getting a glance of his wife, who has her face buried in tissues, "why don't you tell me exactly why you are?"

Cruise nods, seeming perfectly confident despite McIntosh's not so pleasant demeanor. "As your wife Judy explained earlier on the phone, police found your daughter's car abandoned just a few miles from the last place she was seen."

"And that was where?" McIntosh asks, trying his best not to grow impatient.

"A little bar called Cousin Vin's. Have you heard of it?" Cruise asks, glancing at his notes before making eye contact with McIntosh once more.

McIntosh sighs before nodding yes. "It was our favorite spot to go to when she would come home from school. Hell, I even introduced her to it," the doctor states as he begins to move through the foyer, removing his Brooks Brothers sweater jacket and matching scarf before entering in the living room where he is met by Judy, immediately pressing her face into his chest.

Police officers walk around, snooping and clinging together in the room, and McIntosh finds himself eyeballing each one, hoping he doesn't appear nervous or like he is hiding something. "So, have you guys gotten any leads?"

He notices Cruise moving to speak, but the young man is cut off by an older gentleman, about ten years younger than McIntosh, but by the lines in his face, you'd think he was older. "Doctor McIntosh, I'm Detective Russell. We only found your daughter's car a few hours ago. I can tell you that we have not detected any signs of a struggle, but I have my team still working on her vehicle, going over it with a fine-toothed comb."

McIntosh smirks. "How reassuring."

His wife whispers, "Stay calm and be positive. Isn't that what you told me?"

McIntosh kisses Judy's forehead, trying to keep the appearance that he cares for her before meeting Russell's gaze. "So, you're telling me that you have nothing."

Russell looks at Cruise then back at McIntosh and chuckles slightly. "We are working on it, doctor. Did you guys know your daughter was coming?"

The doctor rolls his eyes. "Of course, we did. We expected her this evening."

Russell nods. "So, it seems possible that your daughter arrived earlier today or even in the last two days. Would it be like her to do so and not tell you?"

McIntosh releases Judy as he steps closer to the detective. "I mean, Stephanie is 23 years old. She is an adult, capable of making adult decisions like that. Is this the best you can do? Asking stupid questions like that when you more than likely already know the answer?"

He feels his wife's presence as she places her hand on his shoulder, hoping to ease him. Russell replies, "I am only asking these questions so I, as well as my team, can get a better understanding of exactly who your daughter is."

McIntosh goes to speak but Judy cuts him off, stepping forward in her black dress, her pearl earrings swinging back and forth. "Our daughter has been known to come into town a day or so earlier and she has been known to spend some time with her friends before coming to spend the rest of her time with us. So yes, Detective Russell, you could say that it is like her to show up early and not tell us."

"Thank you, Mrs. McIntosh," Russell says with a smile that the Good Doctor doesn't care for. Russell makes some notes before firing off with another question, "Would either of you be willing to give me and my team a list of names regarding who your daughter spends her time with? Friends, boyfriend, if you know the information, we'd like to have it as it can be a crucial part of our investigation."

Judy sighs as she nods. "Why yes. Of course. Certainly."

As Judy starts to make a list, McIntosh stands up from the couch he found himself resting on and makes his way over to the bar in the kitchen. He begins pouring himself a drink, something he did most nights just to do it. Tonight however, he does it to calm his nerves and so much more. Years ago, he would have never imagined he would be in a situation quite like the one he was now in, but McIntosh tells himself that in this day and age, the worst of the world hitting close to home doesn't seem that out of the ordinary.

McIntosh takes his drink and makes his way upstairs, entering Stephanie's room, which they always keep the same. He looks around at all her trophies and awards, causing McIntosh to smile slightly, feeling that proudness he recalls feeling while staring at her graduation photo downstairs. He reaches the center of the room and for a second, he feels her presence as he whispers, "Where are you, sweet girl?"

McIntosh says a silent prayer, asking God to watch over his little girl. He asks God to please just let all of this be some sort of nonsense. To let Stephanie be okay. To let her be resting peacefully right now on the couch in the apartment of her best friend, Haley. He asks God to just let it be that Stephanie had a little more to drink than she should have and that she was responsible enough not to drive. McIntosh takes a few swigs of his drink, asking God to give him a sign, so he can ease his mind somehow.

A knock startles him, and McIntosh turns to find Detective Cruise standing in the doorway. "Sorry, Mr. McIntosh. I didn't mean to frighten you."

McIntosh wipes his chin, forcing a grin, trying to remember his own advice of being calm. "It's quite alright, detective. It's hard not to be jumpy right now. Being in here right now makes me feel… I don't know… haunted. Oh, it's Doctor… McIntosh."

Cruise lowers his head for a moment, as if he is trying to think of what to say or the best way to approach McIntosh. "You're right. Doctor. I apologize," the detective states, taking a moment to regroup, "In your line of work, do you think you have made enemies?"

The doctor can't help but feel slightly taken aback by the question but does his best to try to mask it, drowning it in his drink. "What do you mean enemies? You do know what I do, correct? I work with people. Mentally ill people, and I help them overcome that illness. I have been very successful."

Cruise nods. "I apologize. I wasn't trying to offend you, Doctor. It was just a question I felt the need to ask, as I don't like to leave any stone unturned, especially when I am trying to help people. I am sure you can understand that."

McIntosh goes to reply, but he refrains. He simply nods as well before turning away. Cruise speaks again, his voice starting to sound far away as he states that he will be in touch.

******

Some time passes before McIntosh finally faces the doorway, seeing that Cruise is gone. He finishes off his drink before pressing his back into the soft mattress of Stephanie's bed, placing himself in the middle of all her favorite stuffed animals that she's kept in pristine condition despite her age, because her father had bought them for her. McIntosh's mind races as he stares at the ceiling, trying to get over the dreadful feeling he's had as Cruise's question repeats over and over in his head like a broken record.

This continues as night turns into day, and McIntosh finally sleeps just as the sun begins to rise.

46

McIntosh goes through his day just as he has been for the last three months since his daughter's disappearance. He is trying to survive. He goes to Trinity, having orderlies like Jeffrey to submit his subjects, his patients, to whatever testing he can devise for them before returning home.

He and Judy, or Judith as she wants to be called now, have separated. The thought of losing their daughter has been too much of a cross to bear. She spends her nights wherever, while McIntosh comes home and drinks alone in the dark until sleep takes over.

Before he leaves, the doctor pays a visit to a few patients on his own. They are in facility X6, the place where all patients eventually go if they fail his tests.

"Evening, Lance," he says, passing by the permanently disfigured creature. He slowly lifts a hand to McIntosh, as it has become his only way to communicate other than grunts or groans.

"Doing well, I see," McIntosh says, trying to appear as gleeful as possible.

He moves on, greeting various patients, before stopping at the last cell on his way out. "Good evening, William. How is life treating you?"

What a waste, he thinks to himself as he sees the toothless William step out from the shadows of his cell. Despite missing all his teeth, the patient has one hell of a wickedly haunting grin. "Evening, Doc. Doing well. How are you?"

"Fantastic as ever," he lies, knowing William's mind is too far gone to grasp that.

William cackles a little. "Very good, very good. You can't lose that, otherwise you'll end up in a place like this."

McIntosh fakes a laugh and smile. "And what's so bad about a place like this? I've treated you fairly, haven't I?"

William nods. "Of course, you have, Doc. You've always treated me like gold. And," he starts, lifting a finger up with enthusiasm as if he has received one hell of a bright idea, "it is good to know that the apple hasn't fallen too far from the tree in that regard."

McIntosh nods and smiles, feeling appreciative of such a comment. "Well thank you, William. I'm leaving for the night. You take care of yourself. I will see you tomorrow."

"You as well, Doc…." William states, slowly returning to the shadows.

McIntosh turns to leave, but something stops him. He repeats William's words back through his mind, feeling a chill run sharply down his spine.

"What did you mean, William?"

The man who murdered his best friend as well as his family looks at McIntosh. That wickedly toothless grin returns. "Whatever do you mean?"

"You said you were glad to see that the apple hadn't fallen too far from the tree? What the hell did you mean?"

"Oh," William states crawling towards him, "I had a visitor yesterday. My first in a long time. It was nice to have a visitor."

"Tell me what I want to know!"

William cackles again, causing the chill in the doctor's spine to melt away into boiling anger. "She was really pretty."

And then, McIntosh suddenly feels dead inside. "She?"

"Yes, your daughter. She said she'd heard about me and wanted to meet me."

"Heard about you? What the… How?"

His grin grows wider. "We have a mutual friend?"

"Who, goddamn you, who?!"

William cackles again, slapping his thigh this time before finally growing eerily silent.

"Tell me who… please…" McIntosh pleads.

William gets closer, almost touching his nose against the doctor's. McIntosh's nostrils sting from the patient's breath as he says, "You'll find out soon enough."

47

It takes all he has, but McIntosh finally reaches his vehicle. He climbs inside, trying to maintain his composure. Taking a glimpse into the mirror, he looks like a ghost. Placing his hands on the steering wheel, he squeezes tightly, telling himself everything is okay.

How does William know Stephanie?

Does he know?

Who is this mutual friend?

McIntosh wants to make sense of it, but nothing adds up.

"I need a drink," he says, clasping his keys in his hand, preparing to put them in the ignition before he catches a glimpse of a gloved hand through the reflection in the mirror.

Before he can react, the back of his head is pinned against the driver's seat. He looks into a pair of eyes that he's seen before, but not for quite some time. The eyes are the last thing he sees before he feels a sudden and sharp pain pierce his neck. He focuses on the eyes for as long as he can.

And then, everything fades.

48

His head spins as he blinks. His ears ring as he blinks, trying to gain his bearings. He blinks until the room comes into focus. It's a white room that he's never seen before. He's in a chair, and across from him, David McIntosh sees a body lying with its stomach to pressed against the floor.

"Look familiar?"

McIntosh feels fear spike throughout his body as he turns to his left, finding James Evans standing in the doorway to the room. He smirks before stepping closer. "I asked you a question, Doc. Does this room look familiar?"

McIntosh shakes his head. "What do you want?"

James rolls his eyes. "No, Doc. I ask the questions. You give the answers. Don't you remember? That was how things worked with us during therapy. Its just that the tables have turned, and now I'm in control of things."

McIntosh sighs, "Why would it look familiar?"

His former patient mockingly groans. "Oh, man. That hurts. I figured you would see it. Maybe you're not as smart as you've always made yourself out to be."

"What the hell are you talking about?"

He grins. "It's not an exact replica, but I think it looks pretty damned similar to the room you had me in when I nearly killed Lance. You remember? The day I beat him to a broken and bloody pulp with my hands. And let's not forget the pipe." James shakes his head before pointing at him. "You didn't forget, did you?"

"What do you want?"

James shrugs. "I will actually answer that, Doc. I figure it's fair." James steps closer to the body on the floor, placing a foot on the lower back before facing McIntosh once again. "I've heard you've had some family troubles. How's that going?"

As soon as he asks, McIntosh gasps, "Please get your foot off my daughter."

James throws his head back and laughs. "It's hilarious that you believe you have any sort of say in this, but you don't."

"GET AWAY FROM MY DAUGHTER!!!"

James removes his foot away from Stephanie and stomps toward him. Before McIntosh realizes, James kicks him in the chest, and he falls back. He gasps for air but James is on top of him, driving his knee into his chest, "Oh, I don't think you can really call her your daughter anymore. She's too far gone. You know, those drugs you gave James... well, if you mix them up all at once..." he cackles again, "talk about a mind fuck."

"But... but you are... James!" McIntosh cries.

He shakes his head. "No, sir. I'm the monster you made. You wanted his violent side. Well, here the fuck I am! The name's Abel." McIntosh feels a bone to bone connection as Abel sends his fist into his nose. "Pleasure to meet you."

Abel pulls McIntosh back up as blood runs down from his nose. Abel walks back toward Stephanie, removing a syringe from his pocket. "What are you doing?"

"Just waking her up. Its time to have some fun," he says before Abel begins to inject her. "You know," he says, glancing at McIntosh from over his shoulder, "you were right. Everyone seems to have a violent side. Your daughter, man, she has been one hell of a fighter. She was, at least, in the beginning."

"She wanted to tear my damn eyes out, Doc. But as time went on, she decided to listen to reason. I told her what I was doing had a purpose. I wanted her to know what sort of fucking monster her father was," Abel states, pulling away the now empty syringe.

McIntosh watches as Stephanie seems to stir, slowly at first, before reverting his attention back to Abel. "James came to me!"

Abel shakes his head. "No. You toyed with his mother. You fed off the hell his father had placed her in. You used James as a goddamn experiment. You scrambled his brain, and you turned him into a monster as well. He couldn't live with his guilt, and now all that is left... is me."

Abel walks out of the room as McIntosh sees his daughter rising to her feet. When Abel returns, he pats her on the shoulder before McIntosh sees what is in his hand.

A lead pipe.

"What are you doing?" McIntosh asks.

"You know, I should really thank you for what you did to James. He's let me in the driver's seat. Who knows when, or if, he'll be back, but…" he trails off before dropping the pipe to the floor. "I was born to protect him, Doc," he says, keeping his eyes locked with McIntosh's. "You hurt him, and you must pay. You must suffer, just as he did, if not worse."

Abel steps back as Stephanie slowly bends down, picking up the pipe. McIntosh's eyes begin to dart back and forth between both before he asks, "Why are you doing this?" Tears stream down his face. Abel wonders if he could taste fear in them if they were to fall on the tip of his tongue.

Abel turns in the doorway as he says, "Closure," and then he steps out, closing the door behind him, as the room fills with McIntosh's screams. He waits, listening to the pain, imagining the man's terror. He waits, every single thud and crack echoes in his brain.

Then there is nothing.

Total silence.

ABOUT THE AUTHOR

Jonah Severin lives in the mountains of North Carolina with his wife and two children. He's worked in the social work field, but writing has always been his first passion. He takes from his experiences and twists them just a little as he brings those stories to life.

NOTE FROM THE AUTHOR

Word-of-mouth is crucial for any author to succeed. If you enjoyed *Dark Fever*, please leave a review online—anywhere you are able. Even if it's just a sentence or two. It would make all the difference and would be very much appreciated.

Thanks!
Jonah Severin

Thank you so much for reading one of our **Psychological Thrillers**.

If you enjoyed our book, please check out our recommendation for your next great read!

The Tracker by John Hunt

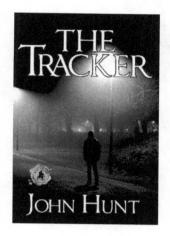

"A dark thriller that draws the reader in."

–Morning Bulletin

"I never want to hear mention of bolt-cutters, a live rat and a bucket in the same sentence again. EVER."

–Ginger Nuts Of Horror

View other Black Rose Writing titles at
www.blackrosewriting.com/books and use promo code
PRINT to receive a **20% discount** when purchasing.

CPSIA information can be obtained
at www.ICGtesting.com
Printed in the USA
BVHW081815200421
605388BV00005B/591

9 781684 336753